Patchwork Poetry & Prose

An Anthology of Writing for Wellbeing

Print Edition
First published 2023 in the UK

Cover design by Kirsty Turnbull
Cover illustration by Angela MacGregor
Illustrations by Claire Harris and Catriona Henderson

eBook ISBN: 978-1-7384741-1-0
Print ISBN: 978-1-7384741-0-3

A catalogue record for this book is available from the British Library.

Special thank you to The National Union of Journalists, The National Union of Rail, Maritime and Transport Workers and The Education Institute of Scotland.

CONTENTS

FOREWORD

FOREWORD

The Matryoshka dolls arranged in descending height in the shop's glass case seemed luminous, the cabinet lights bouncing off their rich red and gold paint like lightning strikes. And with the shafts of light came thoughts about how we are, all of us, dolls within dolls, made up of layers of experience that are buried inside our previous selves. It was a thought I shared with my creative writing classes: characters should have a depth of hidden past experience that influences who and what they are right now.

Babushka, the outer doll, is a grandmother and inside her are all the layers going back to the baby at the heart of the set. When one doll is missing, the set rattles. In that rattle, that all of us surely have, lies our humanity. Our characters need that ill-fitting piece to be believable. If we want to know how our characters might behave, we need to look at ourselves and those we know. Insight, empathy, observation... they are all tools of the writer.

The Matryoshka dolls sparked personal memories: the shy, voiceless child hiding behind her mother's skirt who never lost her insecurity, only disguised it. The teenager who applied 'Pouting Pink' to her lips before sashaying off to lectures. The mother, the daughter, the writer, the teacher: they are all inside me. I asked class participants to do the same: look inside themselves. From my own experience as a novelist, I knew that in those memories and layers, the dreams and insecurities, the light and the dark, were the kernels of fictional stories to be told. Writing is not just imagination; it is experience too.

In the telling of those stories, comes healing. Working with course psychologist, Dr Patrick Lawson, we conducted a study about the effects of using creative writing for mental wellbeing which was subsequently published in *Counselling and Psychotherapy Research*. The results were even more compelling than we dared hope. Participants reported the ways in which wrapping up their biggest challenges in fictional characters and narratives, but retaining an emotional authenticity, helped them process their emotions. They gained valuable detachment, increased insight, and importantly, more self-empathy. Writers found themselves being kinder to their characters who faced their issues than they were to themselves, and began questioning why.

The issues addressed were often serious and dark: domestic abuse; rape; bereavement, including that caused by terrorism; and gender dysphoria. Out of darkness came light. With the invaluable help of individual psychology sessions, participants were encouraged to draw on these experiences, dig deeper into the emotions of them, write about them – and most importantly, process them.

Through the class came a sense of camaraderie and group support. The classes became inspiring, motivating, and fun – because the participants were all of those things. It was my job to get them writing, but their enthusiasm and commitment in turn inspired me to write. One stage of classes turned into two, two into three, and finally, nearly three years later, we are producing our own anthology with the help of our fantastic self-publishing tutor, Ben Galley. We have found stories to tell, and emotions to express, both in prose and poetry.

I could not be more proud of what has been achieved by the group, and their courage in exploring those hidden layers inside themselves. We feel better for writing. We hope you will feel better for reading.

Dr Catherine Deveney, Class Tutor.
Dr Patrick Lawson, Course Psychologist.

WELLBEING

INTRODUCTION

Catriona Henderson

During the dark days of the first Covid-19 lockdown, being able to join an online writing group focused on wellbeing was a ray of light. Organised by the National Union of Journalists and open to members of other unions, the aim was to support the wellbeing of a group of people, many of whom had lost some, or all, of their work. We were an enthusiastic, if disparate, bunch.

As we all learnt the etiquette of Zoom meetings, Catherine led us through a structured approach to working with issues we were carrying, gently but persuasively encouraging us into writing with honesty and bravery. Mixing our own experiences with fiction proved incredibly powerful. For many of us it was cathartic.

We wrote about our struggles from our own perspective, from the viewpoint of others involved in them, and also from that of a neutral observer. Using fiction as a scaffolding to hold key parts of our experiences, we explored imagined highs, lows and resolutions.

Central to the success of this approach was the space that Catherine created. We all felt safe even as we exposed thoughts and feelings that might never have seen the light of day before. Writing our way through anger, fear, grief, despair, satisfaction, happiness and acceptance, we all emerged in a very different place.

Alongside Catherine's steadfast support, another layer of care was in place. Psychologist, Dr Patrick Lawson, had worked with Catherine to develop the structure of the course, and everyone had the opportunity to have a one-to-one session with him. This ensured that anything we had explored through our writing that had been particularly challenging received professional care.

The first wellbeing course was followed by three others, with each of these re-run for other groups of budding writers. The pieces in the wellbeing chapter of this anthology come from these courses, and are sections of work we did to explore our feelings from different perspectives. Some fictionalise our darkest moments as we imagine things getting as bad as they possibly could; others focus on improvements or moving towards our versions of happy endings. Each piece of work has changed the way their authors view their own situations, demonstrating the power of writing.

DEAR THERAPIST

Miriam Landor

As part of the programme, all participants had the opportunity of a one-to-one meeting with a psychologist, an important safety net as we wrote our way through difficult issues towards wellbeing. We were reminded that, "I'm fine," could be an acronym for, "fucked-up, insecure, negative, and emotional..."

Dear Therapist

Dear therapist,

I told you this morning that I was *fine.*

Here's what I should have said...

I don't feel likeable, I don't feel honest.

Fucked-up.

I remember all the mean, shameful small acts I have committed. If you knew those, you wouldn't like me. I don't like myself.

Insecure.

When others seem to like me, it's because I have selected and displayed likeable elements of myself, as you do in social media.

Negative.

I'm being honest here: I'm not an honest person.

Emotional.

In shame, your client.

HERE

Claire Harris

I've had depression for just about as long as I remember. I sometimes wonder how different I would be if I wasn't depressed. I wanted to visualise the depression as an entity I could communicate with, but over the course of writing this and several revisions, the voice of the depression was too strong not to include. It was easy to write how depression manipulates and controls, twisting reality into something it probably isn't. In the end, it's a maze Janet and I are still fighting to leave.

Here

Is it just me, or do you do the same thing to everyone you touch? Make everyone hear the same voices, always questioning ourselves, our experiences, like you do with me? Maybe you plant the same seeds in everyone so we all have similar thoughts. Are you always there, unmoving and constant?

Last night I read depression is a treatable illness, but I've been trying to get shot of you for decades. I don't know what I need to do to get rid of you. You mock my attempts.

Weeks of CBT wasted because I can't switch you off. Journals filled with writings which don't make a dent in you. Mindfulness lessons get close to turning you down for a few seconds. But not completely; no respite from you.

More dedication, better meditation practice, something I can't give to make you go away. You trap me in my head.

Insubstantial in the real world. Things happen around me and I feel like they would be the same whether I was here or not. Let's get this straight: I want to be here. On the planet, in this place, with these people, with y...

Without you.

Will you stay until the end? Living uninvited within me, talking to me and keeping me away from here.

Here? The people I love?

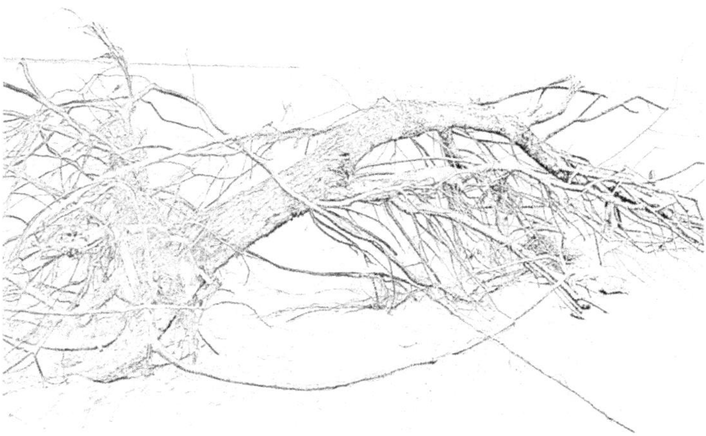

This place. My dark kitchen with its discarded plates, buttered knives and other breakfast detritus casually thrown over the table in the rush to get the kids to school.

The present. Sometimes I hear the seconds of life tick by on the clock, but more often I hear you. The life that happens as I breathe in and out. The reality of listening to the sound of the rain on the window. Here.

I can't feel anything. Emotions are things that happen to other people. Mostly, at least. I can do sad quite well, but I never seem to feel happy in any other place than in the muscles of my face when I smile. You're always there, just underneath, ready to take over and embarrass me with my own tears.

I think it's called masking now. I'm very good at it. Along with compartmentalisation. But these make fragments of me and now I can't be whole. What is contentment anyway?

Wait! It's my turn. Should I say it nicely? I hear what you say, but I feel...

I've learnt from those sessions too.

I envelop you, Janet. I love you, Janet. Without me you would be lost. I keep you safe. When everything else changes in your life, I'm right here, always with you. Everyone knows you're nothing, but I make sure you feel it. How mediocre you are, how average. You don't need a voice. No one respects what you have to say, so it's better not to say anything at all, isn't it? Just keep quiet and let me do the talking. To you, always; inside your head.

You can only be amazing when I am in control.

Emotions are wasted on you. What would you do with those happy thoughts? I make sure you know your value, which isn't much at all. You let me break out of your head into the real world. You let me make decisions.

You don't need food. Food nourishes the body and helps you feel better. No, my way makes sure I'm able to talk to you whenever I want. Let me take away sleep because it turns my volume down.

You want me to stay beside you. Because you're nothing and I make you something.

Shhh, Janet. It's my turn to speak now.

SELF-PORTRAIT

Angela MacGregor

As part of my creative writing course we spent time looking at who we are and what motivates us. As a snapshot of my life, this made me re-evaluate my choices. It is an ongoing struggle to slow down – but being aware definitely helps.

Self portrait

Today, I have finished work already. Up at 4am means lunch by 10.30am and home by 2pm. It's exhausting, getting up so early. This routine fools me into believing I can achieve so much. The sluggishness of my steps and sleep-deprived brain makes every task a mountain to climb.

I am now attempting housework before I go to spend time with my beautiful grandchildren. What a joy they are, a true blessing to my life. This stirs my brain from its slumber as I am energised to finish the cleaning. In the darkened hallway with yet another bundle of washing to do, I pass the old mirror, strangely out of place: a large domineering presence in this enclosed hallway. Strangely, I have no desire to change it as I settle into my new home. It is still, in my mind, my old home. In my reverie, I think I may be like this old mirror. Perhaps the 30-year gap where I experienced the highs and lows of adulthood has brought me back like a circle of life. I retake my place in my childhood home, familiar and alien all at once.

I am snapped out of my thoughts as an image catches my eye. I pause as I realise, I am not alone. My heart is thumping, ringing in my ears. With trepidation, I step back to catch another glimpse. Nah, it can't be. I'm just tired.

Another busy day. I want to accomplish so many tasks and have so little time. Rushing around, as I am prone to do, I think my body is attempting to keep up with the whirring of my mind.

As I try to focus on one task at a time, my brain races on at 100 miles per hour. I am so easily distracted. Oh look! There's my lovely new bright coloured wool. I just bought it in anticipation of my next creative idea. When I picked up my drawing pad and pens, it seemed like for only a moment and now I have lost hours. I should really leave this near the biscuit tin; I might lose weight.

Now where did I leave the dust cloth? Ah that's right, I never made it to the cleaning cupboard before I found a myriad of other activities that are preferable to cleaning. As I start to dust around all the pictures in my hall that tell the story of my life, I can feel my brain drift off, lost in the moment. I attempt to dust the old mirror that's been in this hall my whole life. The hallway is so dark without it. I keep all the doors open to allow as much light in as possible. Looking in the mirror's reflection, I see my family portrait across the hall, from when I was about four years old. That really was a lifetime ago, when we lived in Bridgeton.

I wasn't always in such a great rush. As a young girl, I would spend hours sitting quietly. Coming from a large family, it was great to have a room of my own where I could escape the noise and clamour of everyday life. I always loved drawing or jigsaws but I also loved to sew and knit. My gran had taught me from a young age. We didn't have much, so I would use old clothing or rip up old jumpers. Nowadays, it's called upcycling; back then it was just life.

Don't get me wrong, I could also be one of the noisy ones running, climbing trees or having wild adventures. I think I may be a mix of extreme contradictions. The benefit of lots of siblings was you could always find a companion. At the drop of a hat, you could have someone to do any variety of activities. I loved the fact we could play rounders as we had enough for two teams. It makes me smile when I recall my childhood friend waiting for us to come home. She was an only child and, as our van pulled up (yes, that's right, a van), on return from our summer holidays, Nicola ran down the path and yelled, "The Kennedys are back!" Within minutes, the games had started up once more.

I wonder how many steps I've done today as I rush back through the hall. A reflection catches me by surprise once more. Who is that? How did she get in here? Where did she come from? It's rude to stare. Somehow, I cannot take my eyes away from her. Like one of those toddlers on the bus that look at you unsmiling; you feel the compulsion to pull a face, anything that will provoke a response. I am now that child.

I stare solemnly, intently, into her face. Wild hair twisting out in every direction, escaping the bondage of its clasp. Her eyes are sunken and hardened. The downward turn of her mouth, what sorrow has caused this? Every story etched into her once smooth skin. I hold my breath as if I may hear the secrets contained within the artistry of her face. Wait, those eyes, what is it? I think I might know her. As I continue to look deeper, it's not all as it appears. There it is, a twinkle called hope. I saw it, a glimmer of gentleness, then a twitch of a smile called love. I knew it couldn't be all bad. As my own eyes start to see more and more, I know now it's not all as it appears to be. In fact, she is me.

BEACH BODY

Kirsty Turnbull

The following piece of flash fiction was written as part of the voluntary wellbeing study where we had to write about an issue affecting us (in this case, body image) in a fictional setting. We were a few months into the pandemic when I wrote this, having once again turned to food as a coping mechanism. Only a year or so earlier I had hit my 'goal weight' and I was putting it back on. Clothes started to feel tighter, and the worry of catching the virus didn't make me want to go out and be seen by anyone.

Beach body

When Sophie had bought the bikini, she was feeling confident. It was a royal blue, high-waisted number that had made her feel sexy. But that was months ago. Now she felt exposed, like the bright blue highlighted every imperfection and insecurity. She didn't have much of a choice, though. They were already on their way to their friend's beach birthday party. All that stood between her and the bikini was a matching kaftan. Perhaps she could keep that on all day? A lot of people would be there; no one would notice.

There were already plenty of people on the beach when the taxi pulled up. Music drifted on the light breeze. Annie jumped out of the taxi first, a bottle of Prosecco in each hand. She had on a skimpy bikini and a bumbag. It all fitted her petite frame perfectly. Sophie took a deep breath and followed next, careful to hold the kaftan closed.

"Are you alright?" Mel asked quietly.

Mel had been Sophie's best friend since they were six years old. They were almost like sisters and Sophie found it hard to hide anything from her.

"Yeah," Sophie sighed, "Yeah, I'm alright."

Even over the large round sunglasses, Sophie could tell that Mel had her eyebrow raised at her.

"You look fab, and we're here to have fun!"

Sophie smiled. Mel never lied to her, but she didn't believe she "looked good". They continued down into the party arm-in-arm.

"You're already behind ladies!" Annie said as she approached them with a shot each. Sophie laughed and on three they swallowed the liquid: straight vodka. Annie was never one for starting easy. She gave them a devilish look.

"Much better! Lisa is in there if you wanna go say hi!" and she darted off again towards a large group of topless men.

Sophie and Mel gave each other a knowing look and laughed.

By "there" Annie meant the large beach hut, filled with balloons, presents, people and food. Sophie cast her eye over the sumptuous buffet as they walked in: dainty cakes with pastel icing; perfectly cut sandwiches; mini sausages and pies; vibrant fruit; and as many varieties of crisps and dips as you could think of.

Careful Sophie, she thought to herself, gripping her kaftan again. As she looked up she caught the eye of a man drinking a beer. Was he judging her? Could he see the size of her thighs and stomach? He looked like he worked out. Maybe he was thinking she didn't need it. *Ignore it Sophie,* her inner voice urged.

Lisa was dressed in an extravagant gold swimming costume, a pink, "Birthday Girl" sash draped across her body. She smiled when she saw Mel and Sophie, embracing them both. They chatted and laughed briefly, handing over her gifts.

"We're partying until the sun comes up," Lisa said.

They laughed; the sun had barely gone down yet.

"But you guys *have* to go out on the inflatable obstacle course before you get too sloshed. It's so much fun, like what we used to do when we were kids!"

The local pool had an inflatables night every other week. It was about the only fun thing to do for young teens in their town. They always used to race each other. Sophie wasn't athletic but when it came to swimming back to the start, she always beat everyone.

"Oh we *have to* Sophie! A rematch after all these years!" Mel was determined.

Sophie hesitated.

"You guys were always so competitive at those. It'll be fun! You can leave your stuff here if you like," Lisa said, sipping a pink cocktail.

Mel looked at Sophie expectantly, already dropping her bag and removing her kimono.

"OK," Sophie said, putting her bag next to Mel's, "You're on."

Sophie pulled open the kaftan and slung it off her shoulders. She started to feel hotter. Were people watching her as she left? Could they see the stretch marks on her stomach? Were they disgusted by how much she wobbled? Could they see the red spots of the chicken skin on her arms? Did they think she might stuff something into her face as she passed the buffet table?

Every laugh and every piece of conversation she heard from the beach hut to the shoreline she was sure was directed at her. She kept her arms crossed over her like a shield. Was everyone watching her?

Sophie stopped when the water was hitting her ankles. It was warm, thankfully, and calm.

"Look," she heard someone say quietly behind her, "a whale going back into the ocean."

There was a faint snickering and Sophie looked down at her submerged feet, willing herself not to cry. She felt Mel's arm around her but pulled away, back up towards the hut, away from everyone's gaze.

IN THE DOORWAY

Andrea Pearson

This was one of four pieces written in January 2021. A series of exercises challenged participants to rewrite emotional moments in their life as fiction. I created an alter ego, Khadija, to relive some of my past. Weaving my own memories into parts of her fictional life over those dark winter weeks offered me a creative outlet and injected me with some much-needed emotional buoyancy. While I understand the case against encouraging a middle-class, middle-aged white woman to create a young Arabic woman as a fictional alter ego, quite frankly my only desire was to escape "what I know". Who wants to write about walking through puddles to Morrisons? Khadija gave me sunlit verandas, spicy street markets ... and the chance to think about women facing more than First World problems.

In The Doorway

As she tiptoed through the hall holding her shoe straps, she felt her uncle's presence before she saw his distinctive pot-bellied silhouette. He was sitting in the half-light of his phone, a leg tucked under his bulky behind, crunching sunflower seeds. The large veranda doors were not quite closed and the soft net curtains rippled a little in the night air.

Uncle Iyad was in his late forties, but his hair was already greying and his scrunched oily face made him look older than his years. He had not taken good care of himself – there'd always been others to do that. He was a big figure in all senses and because of his success in property he was well connected with all the right people and, Khadija had heard, a few of the wrong ones too. He was the person the family relied on, to make things happen. Or to make them unhappen.

"Is that you, Khadija?," he said, without looking up.

"Good evening, Uncle. It is good to see you," she said, lowering her head. It was never good to see him.

As the younger of the two brothers, Iyad had moved out when he married, into a villa on the waterfront – apparently it had three kitchens and a basement cinema. But he had never fully left the family home. He was always, somehow, a presence. There every Friday after evening prayers, and always popping into his old bedroom. He'd kept it the same ... all those DVDs stacked up in boxes.

"I wonder where you have been, out so late," he said, skimming his phone onto the seat beside him.

"I was studying... with friends," she replied, standing still under the arched doorway. She hid her shoes behind her back.

After a pause, Iyad manoeuvred his weight off his leg and stretched it out, making him look like one of those marionettes Khadija had seen at the Indian street market.

"Your father tells me you want to go to Paris. Paris? Khadija. Why? What's so good about Paris?"

Her mind played her favourite scene. She would be sitting with friends, girls, and some boys – at a café near the Eiffel Tower. They had laptops and notebooks and were chatting about something, the Mona Lisa, maybe, or the tourists on the Champs-Élysées. The waiter was always the same. Gorgeous. Flirtatious, with all of them, the boys too, but especially with her. He brought them Aperol, and they giggled in the sunshine.

"I have been offered a place at the HEC, Uncle. The Masters programme has a very good reputation. It is number one for business."

"Hmm," he mused. "Reputation is important."

Iyad moved his head to the side and spat sunflower shells into his hand with a pfft, pfft, pfft. Some missed and stuck to the seat. From the kitchen, the fridge whirred as the silence undulated between them.

Suddenly, he ditched the shells, grabbed his phone and got up, pulling back his shoulders and smiling. He took a long stretch and his shirt wafted out over his low-slung waistline.

"Khadija, Khadija, Khadija. You have always been so… spirited. I do have a soft spot for you, I must say."

Her stomach lurched and she felt her top lip tighten as he stepped towards her.

"But why would you want to leave your family? Your mother? This house?" he said, sweeping his arm round in an arc as if this was one of his show homes. "So much fun we had over the years! Do you remember? The parties when you were little, eh? Your brother's birthday, when I bought him that projector. We put up a big sheet in the yard and had popcorn. What movie did we watch? A Disney one I think. What was it Khadija? Do you remember?"

She did remember. She remembered scrunching her dress up to her shoulders; she remembered looking down and seeing her tight bleeding knuckles and her little pants lying beside her feet. Uncle Iyad's face close to hers. His acrid breath, like rotten meat.

He was smiling, singing. "Boop, boop, boop...bare necessities..." Outside, kids were laughing.

"I don't recall," she said slowly. "I must have been too young."

In the distance, a car revved and backfired twice.

"Well," he said as he brushed past her, threading his feet back into his shoes and reaching for the door handle, "We don't think Paris is right for you. You will stay here. With your family."

And with that, it was over.

CATALYST

Indira Mann

Have you ever wondered why a person in an abusive relationship stays with their abuser? I didn't really understand it until I found myself in that situation several years ago. And because I felt I had chosen to be there, it never occurred to me to report him. That's how it is when insanity is normalised. It wasn't until I took part in the Wellbeing Study that I realised how much of that shocking, yet oddly exhilarating, time I still carried around. The following three pieces are fiction that draw heavily on true events. They work in sequence from the impetus to leave, to hope for the future, and, finally, closure. By writing creatively and cathartically about things that happened, I tackled the fear, humiliation and anger that accompanied my memories. I have moved on. I would encourage anyone who has been through a similar experience to try this too.

Catalyst

My stomach churns as the familiar chords of Johnny Cash drift down the corridor. To where I'm perched like a wounded bird on the windowsill, my arms wrapped tightly around my knees to stop the shaking.

The side of my face throbs to the beat of *Folsom Prison Blues* and my mouth twists, somewhat unexpectedly, into a grin. I'm as mad as he is. This 'love' – obsession? – is a prison alright.

I glance down to the street where everything seems so normal and sane. The wine buzz vanished when the adrenalin kicked it and my mind is as clear as the water of Sognsvann. If I stay, I will surely die. So why do I find it so hard to leave?

There's an odd dragging sound getting closer. I can't place it. What was he doing down in the basement? I heard the complaining screech of disused door hinges coming from the hall ten minutes ago.

The door opens and he is there, swaying slightly but anchored to the spot by the weight of the axe in his right hand. You are kidding me. Is this how it ends? A bubble of laughter escapes me before the strange tableau shatters and he lurches towards me.

"What are you doing *here*? I've been looking *everywhere*. Don't. *Ever*. Do. That. Again."

Each word is punctuated by the dull thud of the axe head against the floorboards. This room, my short-lived haven, is rarely used and dust rises up. I should be terrified – that's what he wants – but anger propels me from my perch to a spot directly in front of him.

I shout into his face. "You twisted fuck. How you going to swing that? You can't even stand upright."

He looks down, as the weak winter sun catches the edge of the deadly blade, and drops to the floor. His face contorts with pain now, all traces of anger gone.

"Help me. It's not me, it's this demon. You have to help me get rid of this demon."

God. This is the point where I'm meant to hold him, rocking and soothing: "It's okay, we'll work this out. I'm not going anywhere, it's all okay."

Except this time it isn't. It's the closing strains of a long and disturbing song. From the depths, I've dredged up my last reserve of self-respect. I'm leaving this place and I am never coming back.

Sunset

My creaky digits tuck the tartan wool blanket more firmly about my knees and I make a soft *brrrr* sound as a pale sun drops towards the treeline. There's something about the air today that has unlocked a dusty room of Nordic memories. I close my eyes and step inside.

My career move to Oslo, which lasted a scant two years. Ended just before Christmas when I arrived back in Scotland with two overstuffed rucksacks and a heart full of shards. Nobody was at the airport to meet me – I hadn't told anyone I was heading home. I just wanted to be alone and, for the first time in many months, I got exactly what I wished for.

The newspaper had struck a severance deal with me. I would cover the back shift, my headlines and revisions travelling down the wires from Edinburgh to the chief sub's screen. My old life caught up with me early in the new year in the shape of several large boxes strapped to a wooden pallet.

As I set about forming an alternative future – free from the tyranny of a man who thought control was love – sometimes, the pain of loss would cut me in half. On those nights, I would sift through hundreds of frames capturing our treks into the Norwegian wilderness: ancient landscapes strewn with rocks hurled there by giants; endless forests; and the deep, dark waters of the lakes, where the monster Draugen lies in wait for unwary children.

I filtered, cropped and adjusted image after image and, as I did, the memories connected to each lost their sting. These places did not belong to him; he just happened to be there while I framed their timeless beauty.

Slowly, I came to realise these photographs held a deeper purpose – a pathway to another life, and livelihood. I showed some to a friend and she agreed, suggesting that I combine the images with words describing my one true love: the power of nature.

I surprised myself as well as others by dedicating my first book to him. Through him, I glimpsed the wild heart of his mother country and that gave me the courage to explore many more hinterlands.

A slight movement at my elbow rouses me and my eyes snap open. My daughter has set down a cup of hot chocolate and, very wisely, left me to my thoughts. She was – and still is – the crystal that brought me back to the light all those years ago.

I shift slightly in my chair. I may not be as sprightly as I once was but the cold does not bother me too much, and I sit here most days until the daylight fades. I raise the camera's viewfinder slowly to my eye and frame the stark silhouettes of branches against a peach melba sky. *Click*.

Closure

Dear ____

You will be as surprised to read this letter as I was to find myself writing it. Are you even still alive? To my mind, there were two paths facing you: you cleaned up your act, or you checked out early at the hands of a lover's enraged husband. Perhaps a third reality, where you finally went too far and surrendered your liberty?

Should I have stayed and tried to save others from your questionable charms? I don't think so. Your family knew what you were and did nothing. Said nothing. Even your former girlfriends, left battered and blue, lived in utter denial. In the face of such insanity, it was right to come home.

I always thought it rather trite to say that time is a great healer. But it turns out to be true. And I want you to know this – and to read these words again until you get it – I didn't love you. You were just an escape hatch to a better life. I can picture your ego right now, foaming at the mouth, furious and appalled.

When I came back to my beloved Scotland, the hurt and the fear receded as real friends encircled me with their care. But that is now ancient history. In this envelope, you'll find a book and some of its images will be rather familiar to you. Actually, all of them. So maybe, after all, there was a reason for "us". That, and learning the hard way what true love really is.

Goodbye ____, and may the Devil cut you some slack.

BOAT

Donna Macaulay

This piece of flash fiction was written in response to an event witnessed by the writer.

Boat

"My brother is on the boat too."

The words sank from the rawness of her mouth to the pit of her stomach and then to her shaking knees.

The bomb is planted directly below where Matthew stands at the wheel. The day is beautiful. The sea a blanket of deep calm. He can see Urchin Island, fulmars on the cliff and the reef beyond, where a cormorant stands motionless with outstretched wings. Gannets are diving, streamlined arrows to their targets. The hull of the boat chugs constantly steady, in its wake a frothing white tail outstretched behind.

The buoys marking his lobster pots are red. The lobsters crawl within the rope meshes of the pots below, unable to exit through the entrance which enthralled and then enticed them towards a certain death. The rock is coral pink and studded with anemone and urchins and starfish. Kelp sways. Fish shoal in silver flashes and the shrimp and crab scavenge. A fine underwater balance poised as the tide pushes and pulls.

He is relaxed, steering towards the first haul of pots. The sky is a clear blue as the boat slows. He can taste the salt on his lips; the breeze ruffles his hair. Sea molecules are freshly bursting in his nostrils and a gannet infused with power and grace is crying with raucous vibrato. He glimpses the white and black and gold of her feathers as she wheels and turns.

Her wingspan is difficult to judge in free flight. It can be up to 180 centimetres. Her sharp eyes can detect prey underwater, amid the refracted and reflected light where air and water meet. He wishes his eyes had that acuity. She strikes the water like an arrow. Her skull is adapted to withstand tremendous force. She can see clearly underwater. Her beak clamps down on a fish and she bobs up to shake the fish and swallow it whole, readying herself for the ascent to dive again. She is a combination of beauty and lethality.

The force of the bomb rips his jeans, ravages his limbs, tears off his little finger. The gannet wheels high above the exploding mass of blood and flesh and bone falling to the turmoil below.

Her memory of that day, from the moment the bomb exploded, is a series of still images. A film with no coherent narrative.

DIFFERENT SEASONS

Catriona Henderson

The first wellbeing writing course was during the height of Covid-19, and I learnt such a lot by writing about elements of my reality in a way that wasn't constrained by them. It was the perfect thing to be doing when many things were so obviously out of our control. By exploring how I would feel if my fiction was happening, I could take things I was struggling with and develop them in contexts that were, at times, completely different to what I was actually dealing with. One of the great benefits of this was being able to write freely as no one, other than me, would ever know which parts are based on fact and which are completely fictitious. I have continued to use writing to support my wellbeing and find huge value in this.

Different Seasons

It's three months since you were diagnosed with cancer. Breast cancer. You still find it hard to say those words, but maybe it's becoming slightly easier with time as familiarity takes root. There are also harder things to say.

We chart your journey through the plants in your garden. The walks you had enjoyed are no longer possible as the cancer flourishes, spreading like the runners of the strawberry plants you'll probably never see bear fruit again. The spring flowers have shared their optimism for the year ahead through yellows, purples and blues, mirroring the reaction of your arms to the endless invasions of needles and medication. They shone and passed, but your bruises developed into the dark purple hues of Veronica, the irony of its everyday name of Speedwell contrasting with your own demise.

You restrict the flowers in your garden to a small palette of colours. If you could, you would have banished green as you did from every other part of your life, having loathed it since your bottle green school uniform of high school, but nature refuses to offer this as a possibility so green remains with a tenacity even greater than your grudges. Now your garden mirrors the shades of your skin, and if you did ever wear green you'd be perfectly camouflaged. As you visibly start to wither, the opulence of summer explodes and, with it, a different energy.

I call you, expectations low. As usual this is unlikely to be a conversation, more an interview of obligation as I ask you the same questions and get the same answers. "How are you feeling today?" And although you have even less to talk about than before, I find I'm actually interested in the answer. Partly it's because there's not much longer to go before we're both released from this uncomfortable duty resulting from the bonds of family. But maybe your cancer is changing both of us. Anger is still there. Your unwavering rebuttal of any offers of help, that means we lurch from crisis to crisis, has seen my frustration at how much easier life could be, grow rather than diminish. Something else has grown too, though. A respect for your determination has appeared, as if a seedling has grown unexpectedly and escaped the usual weeding of alien interlopers.

"I'm doing fine. Nice to see the irises out. I was worried the wet winter would have killed them. How are you? It must be hard juggling work with the kids."

It's the first time since I left home almost thirty years ago that you have asked me how I am or acknowledged that I might work hard. You don't even know what job I do, and the few other comments you have made about my children have been focused on how wonderful their dad is, his parenting outshining anything I could do. I am so unused to sharing anything of my life with you that I feel myself tense and recoil, as if this an attack rather than an invitation. It certainly feels like an intrusion.

There are so many means of defence I have learnt from you that this opening in your barricades is a shock. But maybe for this final stage in our journey a different path is a possibility. After all, what is left to lose?

So, I tell you about the kids and my work, even though a part of me still feels you don't deserve to know, and you listen and manage not to argue with me. You even ask a few other questions. It's almost a conversation.

Later sitting in my own garden, which is a defiant riot of colour, I realise that what I feel is relief. Relief that things might still be different even if it's only for a short while, and comfort that maybe there is space for me and my family in amongst the plants you have so carefully nurtured. Amongst the flowers, I notice the tinge of autumn colours, as the first plants start to make their transition while others are still coming into bloom, and take comfort that we're moving into a new season.

THREE AND A HALF HOURS

Keith Davidson

In February 2017 my elderly father was taken to hospital with significant vascular disease. More than five months later, after amputation, recovery and rehab in three different hospitals, he came home.

Since the death of my mother, dad had been living quietly and capably on his own for several years. By summer 2017, that all changed. There was a care plan, carers, a wheelchair, a prosthetic leg and myself splitting my time between my flat in Edinburgh and the old family house in Banff.

Dad had more spells of hospitalisation later in 2017 and into 2018; I spent more and more time with him, coordinating his health and social care, running the household, communicating with the care company, with the NHS, and keeping family up to speed.

In spring 2019, I officially moved in with him. By then, he had been diagnosed with mixed dementia, albeit in mild form.

For letting off steam, for therapy, for unwinding, I blogged about dad and care on social media – just among family and friends. When I found out about the Creative Writing For Wellbeing course, I thought, I'm already doing that, sort of. It was a natural fit.

In this section of the anthology, there are two pieces I wrote in the summer of 2019: one relates to a June morning where writing allowed me to think my way out of a bad mood; the other is about a hellish twelve days in July.

I lived with my father until he died in November 2021, aged 87.

Three and a half hours

0650

Alarm goes off. I swing out of bed, stick on a shirt, then blearily try to get my legs into a pair of jogging bottoms.

Dad shouts my name.

"Uh, dad?"

I open the bedroom door, still trouserless, to ask if he's okay. He heard my alarm, presumably, and me footering about, getting dressed. His bedroom is opposite mine, across a narrow hallway; he sleeps with the door wide open.

On waking up, I'm less than five metres from the mouth shouting my name.

"I had an accident with the yoo-rine bottle," he says.

He apologises. I say it's okay and try to sound reassuring.

The carpet by his bed has a small circle of piss. Such bedroom spillage does not happen often but it does happen occasionally. If he needs to pee in the night there are urine bottles on his bedside cabinet. Doziness at 2am or 3am can easily mean a misdirected stream of urine or a spilled bottle. I make a mental calculation about the cleaning up, the imminent arrival of the carer, the notion of three people in one bedroom – one woman in a blue smock, one elderly man with restricted mobility and myself with a bucket – and decide to sort the matter once dad is up and in the living room. I get my jogging bottoms on then head for the front door, unlock it, then to the kitchen. Kettle. Coffee.

0700

The carer bowls in, largely perky and professional despite the hour. We cover, "hello"; "the rain has stopped"; and, "mind the wet carpet"; then she goes to attend to dad. Almost immediately, the base unit for the community alarm pings on, like a freakishly loud modem from 1996. In sitting up from his bed, dad has dinged the alarm on his wrist which has a fairly sensitive impact sensor. This connects to the base unit and the base unit connects to a control room in the aether.

Soon a voice issues forth, "That's your community alarm. Is everything alright?"

Dad and the carer are at the other end of the house, so I stand by the unit, tell the voice that it was a false alarm, thank you, and nothing to worry about. They ping off.

Okay, this time, coffee, modest cafetière, but before I can pour a cup the base unit for the community alarm pings on again. The carer laughs, dad says something about throwing his wrist alarm out the window, I stand by to tell a different voice that, no, dad's fine, it was another false alarm.

0710

I go and hide in the spare bedroom, also known as the study, with coffee. I play Boom Beach on my phone for a while, invade some islands, blow some shit up. Around ten minutes later, once I hear dad and the carer bimble down the hallway, I go and get a bucket, a scourer, some cleaner, then scrub the pissy stain in dad's bedroom. But I need Vanish too, for its aerosol tin has aliphatic hydrocarbons, anionic surfactants, polycarboxylates, phosphates and perfume. Plus, when you skoosh it on the carpet it's kind of cool the way it gets all foamy.

The tin is under the kitchen sink. It feels nearly empty. It is empty. I make a mental note to buy some more Vanish.

0745

The carer's duties all done, she heads off. I wander into the living room to have a chat with dad. I am mostly thinking, 'That's the piss cleaned up,' and 'Breakfast!'

"We going to the barber then?" dad asks.

Over the last few days he has been asking about a haircut – he does need one. It has been raining heavily, however, so leaving the house in such weather, never mind manoeuvring into the barber shop, has seemed too daunting. No rain today, though.

What I'm thinking is, "Fuck's sake, give me a minute, I've just sorted out your wet carpet and I've not even had breakfast yet."

What I say is, "Uh, right, I'll get breakfast and then we'll see… Yeah. Not raining. Be fine. Breakfast. Uh."

I go and get something to eat then scutter with aplomb. Some of the scuttering even has purpose: cleaning dishes, portioning up some soup I made yesterday, putting it in the freezer. Some of it involves invading islands and blowing shit up.

0915

Move car in driveway so that the passenger door is near the wheelchair ramp rather than opposite side. Pack dad's specs, mobile and wallet into a bag. Lock back door, etcetera. Off we go.

Dad takes his wheelchair out the front door, down the ramp to the car passenger door. He stands up, using the open passenger door for support – I hold it steady and stop it swinging – then he turns and sits gingerly down on the car seat.

This is now one of the very rare occasions when dad's wheelchair is neither in his bedroom at night nor occupied by day. I sweep off some crumbs, take the cushion off, shake it, sweep off further assorted detritus under the cushion, then notice some tomato ketchup stains. I pop back into the house, get a wet scourer, clean off the dried tomato ketchup, put the scourer back, deposit the wheelchair with cushion in the hallway, lock the front door then jump in the car.

The drive takes less than five minutes; it's not much more than a mile. Dad's walking frame is in the back seat so he can get from the car into the barber's. The main man at the shop sees us park up directly outside his door. He knows dad and is aware of his mobility issues. He comes out to help, genuine and friendly. Given the barber's is on a steep, pedestrianised brae...

Interlude

People sometimes ask, "Why don't you write more?" Part of the answer is that I got so far with the text above – not quite a thousand words – then the next carer turned up around ten minutes early for the 11:45 visit, with her chatty, high-impact style which made it literally impossible to sit at the kitchen table and focus. Dad has now had a mince and onion pie for lunch, with beans; two paracetamol have been necked. While that was going on I refilled all three bird feeders and re-potted a plant. Dad is now settled, fed and in front of Keeping Up Appearances. It's not yet noon.

0915 continued...

...dad has to swing out of the car, stand up with his walking frame, walk a short distance laterally across the brae, up a step then into the shop. He does this with the supervision of both myself and the barber. No problems to date. Safely inside, I abandon him. The car is blocking the brae so it really is just a matter of unloading dad then moving on.

I head for Tesco, buy dad a Press & Journal and get some groceries. Afterwards I park up on the foreshore and watch the sea.

0955

My phone goes. The barber tells me that dad is ready for uplift. A few minutes later I'm back at the shop, blocking the brae again with the car. Usually by this point in a barber's visit, dad is sitting by the door in the waiting area. He has paid and is all ready to go. This morning, he's still in the barber's chair and hasn't paid. I get his bag, take some money out of his wallet and hand over the notes. By this time, the barber is attempting to get dad to stand up from the chair and is struggling – this is happening across the shop floor from where I am.

Dad isn't so much standing up as the barber is picking him up. Both myself and another customer make moves towards dad and the barber when we see what's going on. I get there first – having paid – and with the combination of the barber's lift, my assistance and dad's own effort, he gets vertical. Both myself and the barber supervise dad out of the shop, over the lip of the doorway, down the step, the few paces across the brae to the car door, then into the passenger seat.

As we set off, dad is puffing like an old horse with the effort of standing up and walking a few metres, not all on the level; I'm driving carefully down the narrow brae, hazards on, past another wheelchair user, focused on not causing death by motor vehicle. Once back out on to the main street at the bottom, having given Ms Wheelchair as wide a berth as I could, I point the car in the direction of home.

"We going to the baker?" says dad impromptu, eyes on the prize of a mince and onion pie. Swear words pass through my mind.

"Yeah, fine," I say. I drive to the baker, leave dad in the car, get a mince and onion pie then jump back in the car and start driving again.

"And can we get a paper?" he says.

"Already got one," I say. My pre-emptive Tesco purchase.

Within minutes we're back at the house. I retrieve his wheelchair from the hallway, position it at the car door. He swings his legs out, stands up using the door for support – me bracing it as usual – then turns round and sits down. I push the wheelchair plus dad up the ramp to the house door, across the threshold and into the hallway. He can take it from there.

1020

He soon trundles off to the loo. As he comes back, past the kitchen, I ask if he wants a coffee. He says yes. Coffee made, I glance at the time – I've been up for three and a half hours. And I didn't get Vanish at Tesco.

Later

The point in writing this, I guess, is that it takes me round the houses to a conclusion. I got up before 07:00 today and even before I was fully dressed, I had a piss-cleaning task in my in-tray.

Before I had breakfast, dad was asking me to drive him to the barber, which means a great deal more than simply driving him to the barber.

Before we got home he was asking me to stop off somewhere else that I should doubtless have anticipated and – when we did – there would have been one more call had I not already bought a newspaper.

"What the fuck is this? Drip-feed request day?" I didn't say.

Yeah, I was tetchy.

But given the dementia, he never is going to wake up and present me with a list of wants: barber, baker, paper shop. Even if he did write a list he would probably forget that he had done, or where he put it.

On reflection, beyond all my knee-jerk grump, this was him behaving like a normal human being again: getting up, fancying a trip to the barber, thinking that he could stop off at the baker, then remembering he could pop in by the paper shop and get a Press & Journal. It was the old dad, the way he used to be before hospital more than two years ago, acting on impulse but with me as an enabling device.

It was therefore a good morning, even though it's not always easy being an enabling device.

Writing is better than blowing shit up.

TWELVE DAYS IN SUMMER

Keith Davidson

On the morning of Friday 12 July, I was in town. I went to see Aberdeen play Rovaniemi in the Europa League the night before, stayed over with brother and sister-in-law, then planned a leisurely drive back up the road. But a carer called me around 8:20am to say she was worried about the condition of dad's right leg so had summoned medical help. Someone was coming to see him later in the day.

I drove straight home. Dad seemed generally okay although his right leg, prone to oedema, was red and swollen. It often is. He said he was fine. He always does.

An advanced medical practitioner arrived at lunchtime and prescribed antibiotics to combat a leg infection: cellulitis. I collected the meds from the local pharmacy and dad started the course. It was noticeable that his appetite was slightly off.

By Monday 15 July, there was clearly something wrong. There were complaints of stomach pains. The next day, he was keeping a basin by his wheelchair in the living room in case he threw up.

Come Wednesday 17 July, he wasn't eating at all and went back to bed in the afternoon. His blood sugar had also spiked, not to levels that would cause panic for a mild diabetic like himself, but certainly higher than usual. I called the advanced medical practitioner for advice and she popped up to the house. The advice was to finish the course of antibiotics for the leg and to submit a urine sample.

On Thursday 18 July, the advanced medical practitioner called to say the urine test showed a urinary tract infection. This meant more antibiotics. Dad was too weak and ill to get out of bed at all and still not eating. Around this time, pardon the vagueness, there was also a prescription for meds to settle his stomach.

Come Friday 19 July, his right leg was looking much better. The initial course of antibiotics seemed to have sorted the cellulitis. Dad was still stuck in bed though, weak, not eating, not drinking nearly enough water and complaining of stomach pains and sickness. The situation persisted over the weekend. He did get up on the Sunday, although that proved a little premature.

By Monday 22 July, the advanced medical practitioner called to say that further results from the urine test suggested a better kind of antibiotic to deal with dad's urinary tract infection so stop the meds he'd been taking since the previous Thursday and collect some new ones. He did get up for a while but was too weak and sickly to stay up so went back to bed again.

On Tuesday 23 July, by pre-arrangement, I left dad sleeping after breakfast while I drove a few miles along the coast to see a mate. I was away for two hours. When I got back, I found that dad had suffered a peeing accident with a urine bottle, in bed, but was too weak to get up and do anything about it. He had been lying in the wet for around an hour.

He was completely done, scunnered. Even thinking back more than two years to when he was sent to hospital, the amputation, rehab and all the rest of it, he never seemed so down and defeated as he did right there and then. But the bed and dad got sorted – with the help of the 11:45am carer.

Many things had to be washed – bedding included – so dad went to sit in the living room in his wheelchair for a while. At some point in the afternoon he shifted from the wheelchair to the settee for a change of position, something more comfortable. Very unusual. The problem? He couldn't get up from the settee unaided. I knew what might happen but his motivation levels were less than zero. Once he'd plonked himself down, I had no chance of shifting him voluntarily.

The inevitable happened. By the time he realised he needed to go to the bathroom, there wasn't enough time for me to physically haul him to his feet in his weakened condition, get him back into the wheelchair, reach the bathroom and supervise him on to the loo. The fact that his prosthetic leg fell off en route, just as we were going through the living room door into the hallway, didn't help. Comedy in the dark moments?

"I need the loo! I need the loo!"

Klonk.

Yeah but your leg's just fallen off and the wheelchair won't go over it. I'll have to pull you back into the living room, walk round you, pick the bloody leg up, stick it back on you, then push you to the bathroom, I thought. No point in saying.

It all took too long so he wet himself as we reached the bathroom. More laundry. Dad's mental state was not helped by lack of fluids and it being the hottest day in this part of the 'shire since dinosaurs roamed the Earth.

When the 4:15pm carer came she managed to get dad to test his blood sugar. It had spiked again to call-the-GP levels. I phoned the surgery. They said they'd send someone up to the house the next day.

With clean sheets on the bed, but still no food being eaten, dad went away back to bed around teatime. I stuck my head round the door from time to time to check on him. At the back of 9pm, I did a routine glance, saw him awake, asked if he was alright and he told me he'd wet the bed again, another dropped and spilled pee bottle accident. He could have summoned me with a shout but didn't even try – he had just lain in a slightly wet bed for 15 or 20 minutes? Maybe half an hour.

I got that partly fixed – fitted sheet off, waterproof mattress protector cleaned and dried, carpet skooshed with Vanish – but waited for the 10pm carer to come before finishing off. Putting a clean fitted sheet on a bed for a very tired and weak 84-year-old, or replacing the duvet cover, is easier with two. Thankfully the carer came a little early so dad was soon settled in a dry bed once more.

The carer left. I flopped on the settee to unwind with a gin. The more stressful the day, or 12 days, the longer the decompression period.

On Wednesday 24 July, we were almost back to normal. Dad had a shower, got up and accepted a coffee. First hot drink in some time. He felt slightly better, he said. Perhaps the effects of the second lot of antibiotics for the urinary tract infection were kicking in.

Moral of the tale? As a man with early stage mixed dementia, mild diabetes, one leg and vascular problems, dad generally does okay as long as nothing else intrudes. Throw a couple of infections, plus three different lots of antibiotics into the mix – with an attendant upset stomach and no appetite – and it very quickly becomes obvious just how vulnerable and helpless he can be, how his decision-making goes completely off-beam. There were times over the last 12 days when dad literally couldn't sit up in bed.

From the care perspective, day 12 was toughest, even with four care visits from the professionals. The fact that the drugs had led to an improvement offered some light at the end of the tunnel, but by then I thought an air-conditioned hospital room, 24/7 care and a drip to get fluids back into him would have been better than being at home.

The other moral of the tale is don't watch old, unseen Christmas episodes of Doctor Who late in the evening after circumstances such as these. They just make you cry.

MO WINS GOLD

Lois Houghton

In 2012, at the age of 44, I was diagnosed with breast cancer. This piece tells of the impact that the London Olympics had on me while I was going through a tough year of surgery, chemotherapy and cancer treatment. My parents were both marathon and ultra distance runners and I have always been inspired by the dedication and sacrifice needed to achieve in sport. I have watched the video clip of Mo Farah winning Olympic Gold hundreds of times and whenever I am facing a physical or other life challenge, I play it in my mind. They are my cheerleaders!

Mo Wins Gold

Her mind awoke before her eyes opened. For the first glorious few seconds, she didn't know where she was or what had happened. Those first few blissful seconds of nothing. An empty mind, just her heartbeat and breathing. Peace.

Then one by one her senses awoke as the general noise and hubbub of her surroundings crept in. The beeps and whirring of the heartrate monitors, the gentle hum of the air conditioning, the clatter of crockery on the tea trolley with the wonky wheel. The chatter of the nurses at shift change, recounting stories of their long-awaited, they-went-too-fast, days off. Stories of arguments with boyfriends, bad experiences of poor service at restaurants, and the man on the bus at work with bad body odour. Stories of mundane everyday life. A life she would trade anything for at that moment. Even the unpleasant, mundane, everyday life. A life she didn't know how she would get back to.

She kept her eyes shut just for a few more precious seconds before she let in the bright fluorescent light, then became aware of the feeling of pressure in her bladder. That horrible feeling that in real life, home life, you get when your alarm is due to go off in 10 minutes. You kid yourself on you can ignore it. Ignore it for a few more minutes in the warmth of your bed. She really, really, needed to pee.

She gingerly turned her head to look for the toilet door. It was only about 20 feet away but it may as well have been 20 miles. She looked at the drains coming from her stomach and chest, her chest distorted and flat where her breasts used to be, the bags of fluid she would have to carry with her. Every bit of her hurt. She had never felt so helpless. She would never again take for granted the simple luxury of being able to go for a pee. She looked again at that mountain she had to climb, and for a few short moments wondered what would happen if she just wet the bed.

I can't do it; I just can't do it. It's too hard, too far. Then she started to cry.

She had fallen asleep with the small bedside TV showing the coverage of the 2012 London Olympics. Feats of outstanding physical achievement, personal sacrifice, lives dedicated to preparation and training. She wondered to herself how she could have trained and prepared for this. This fear, this pain, this life challenge.

The familiar North East tones of Brendan Foster commentating registered in her consciousness. Mo Farah was competing for a gold medal in the 1000 metres. Through her drowsy drugged haze, she remembered that Mo Farah had gone to the same school as her; he had always been one of her sporting heroes. How different their lives were. As the excitement rose in Brendan's voice, she became absorbed in the race and for a few short minutes she forgot her pain.

"The big kick has started and he looks dangerous to me in third place."

For a few short minutes she forgot about the last three months of hospital appointments, scans and biopsies.

"Mo Farah is gritting his teeth now, the arms have got to pump, the knees to come up high."

For a few short minutes she forgot about the pitying looks, people not knowing what to say so saying the wrong thing.

"He's got to find something extra! He's got to kick hard! COME ON MO FARAH!"

For a few short minutes, she forgot about people telling her she was brave when she didn't feel it.

"Farah is going to make it! Two Gold medals for Great Britain, BEAUTIFUL! He's the double Olympic champion!"

The cameras then switched to Denise Lewis and Colin Jackson in the studio, standing on their chairs, jumping, arms in the air, screaming for Mo to win. Screaming words of encouragement, the cheers and dreams of a nation behind them, tears of joy.

He had done it. Mo had won!

Then through the emotion, the elation, back to the hospital ward, back to her hospital bed and the realisation that her bladder was still full. She still really, really, needed to pee. She looked across the vast chasm to the toilet door and began to shift herself to the edge of her bed, slowly gathering up the drains, pulling the oxygen monitor from her finger. Putting her foot onto the floor, the first step.

This time she felt, for the first time, that with Brendan Foster commentating on her progress across the ward, and Denise and Colin cheering her on, she might, just might, be able to get through this.

SAFE SPACE

Angela MacGregor

Come, take a breath or two, maybe more, as I close my eyes and capture it again. If I squeeze my eyelids tight, it creates beautiful colours of greens, yellow, pinks. It is similar to a sunny day as the rays penetrate your eyelids, dazzling you in technicolour. Ah there it is, now relax.

Another deep breath, as I take in the vista, once more. Not a cloud in the sky all the way to the horizon where it meets the crystal-clear ocean of topaz. It's so warm here! The tiniest breath of wind brings the salty scent of the ocean before me, offering some light relief from the heat on the beach. Maybe I will paddle but not yet.

Tentatively, I step barefoot onto the warm sand. It is soft, like talcum powder, delicately enveloping my toes.

Just a few small steps. It's not far to reach the hammock by the palm tree. You slowly look around this deserted beach that stretches for miles. Away in the distance, as the island peaks beyond the bay, I see a bird cruising the thermals by the mountains. It's nothing more than a small black blob from here, impossible to identify. Seeing it soar wild and free is enough for me.

As I lay back in the hammock, it sways me from side to side, in rhythm with the ocean. I take another breath and close my eyes. I hear the wind as it sings me its lullaby in the palm leaves above. Whispering its love song like a balm to my soul, "rest awhile". I realise all is right with the world once more. This is my beach and I can share it with you.

POETRY

FINDING MY WAY BACK TO THE OCEAN

Gillian Bowman

there's light on the surface: falling
the cracks are showing;
my body fights, not knowing
the movement in the ground

patience. I was tied, lying
In the waiting, enduring,
searching, shattering, fracturing,
then I see

white corridors, waiting, crying, the cold
goodbyes at midnight, last sip of water, last hope
last words, last hand I hold
falling into an abyss with no way out

I close my eyes. Wading,
hurting, washing my face with grief
falling, cold water, my self fading
into murky depths.

a hand reaches out.
it is mine. I am there before me.

come with me to the ocean

by the stars on a clear night
it wasn't your fault
my body shatters, scattered into the waves.

THE DEAD ARE HAUNTED

Sam Phipps

The dead are haunted
by the living,
they don't understand
who we've become –
sometimes it's us sending
shivers through them.

My father visits me at night,
he frowns, longing for
resolution –
my mother leans in low,
as if listening out
for my heart.

FISHER DAD

Donna Macaulay

The flies you tied are double cast
In deep pools of your memory:
Blue Flash Damsel Gold-head,
Pheasant Tail Nymph Blue,
Catch of brown trout, rainbows,
All the loughs you fished.
Netted steadfastly too,
The names of those you love,
In a mesh of hardwired passion.
Yet, the words you utter vanish,
To where your gaze lingers,
Smudged in a watery distance.
And the words you hear, dissolve
Swiftly, to a muddle of churned
Consonant and vowel.
You plant a dry stick and water it,
You dig in the earth for apples,
You pull the heads off random flowers,
And get lost, so lost on the path.
You stare at Whirligig beetles,
On a summer's day, spiralling madly,
Gleaming bronze on the lake.
Why are they swimming in circles?
Making ripples, I say.
Why are they swimming in circles?

Seeking prey, I say.
Why are they swimming in circles?
I don't know, I don't know, I say.

THE FARMER

Lois Houghton

Deep lined hands
Like furrows on the land
Fingers gnarled with time
Carved from memories

A furrowed brow
Pushing the plough
Bent against the wind
In the tracks of his father

Muck on his boots
Supported by the twisted roots
Sheltered in the shade,
Of the family tree

Hands that plant the seeds
Hold the child he feeds
Teaching him to grow
A father's love

BRASS ELEPHANT

Donna Macaulay

My little sculpted treasure,
Iced in burnished yellow.
Your trunk proudly aloft.
You played in wild jungles
Of dock and dandelion
And on dry paved banks
Of cracked tiles and poker.
You foraged dense thickets,
Munched on plumpest catkin,
Pollen on your brass rump
And you rolled happily
In beds of pussy willow
Of a true elephant grey.

You resided long on sills,
Overlooking a dreary view,
Or the warm fire hearth
Sometimes centre prided
On rounded doily lace
Crowning the Queen's table.
You nestled often too in
The warm curl of my palm.
A nugget of pure gold,
I rubbed you with lint to
Shine you to pale sunlight.

You stand on my fireplace,
Facing north trumpeting,
The dust motes layering,
Settling on Grandma's eyes
Peering glassily, warm
From the heart of the frame.
I hear her whisper echo
In the chamber, as Fionn
Clasps you squealing, in his
Pudgy palm, astonished
By your ponderous feel.
His delight redrafted,
Scribed alpha, omega,
Her great-great-grandson.

CANCER MOON

Tina Norris

Today the milk-white breast of the matter.
I cannot cradle you,
your knees tucked under your chin
on your Swansea sofa,
so I open my laptop.
There is treatment, I say,
but no guarantees.
You peer at me through the screen
as you used to study a dandelion
before blowing the seeds
into the evening sun.
And so? you ask.

My eyes are red,
scratchy like the back of currant leaves.
We lie, moon-swaddled,
in separate cities,
staring at the ceiling,
wondering if this tide is neap or spring.
The laptop pulses dead-star light
through the early hours.
I dream you are five again.
Summer heat wraps the apple tree
where the old swing hangs between echoes.
A-tishoo! A-tishoo! We all fall down.

BITTER SWEET

Lois Houghton

And she's walking, very slowly
through treacle
dragging her back to the trees.
He's treacle, sickly sweet
he brings her to her knees.
The sweetness is burning
bitter in her mouth
he's shouting, she's crying
Help me please.
And she's walking, very slowly
he's dragging her back
with sweetness, bitter burnt sugar
he's stroking her ankles
tightly
pulling her back.
And she's walking, very slowly
forwards
through treacle
not looking back.

KNIGHT AND DAY

Angela Kennedy

I saw you like a knight in shining armour
Strong and brave, mighty, safe.
I knew now I could finally be
loved and cared for, finally me.

Why, then, would you hurt me so?
I loved you – didn't you know?
Hold my breath, be deathly still
Pray he'll stop, bend his will.

I see it now, your armour rusting and broken
My love... your hatred... choking.
How did I not notice it, way at the start?
You could not save me, or love my heart.

It's time to say I have to leave
Carrying no regrets for you, for me.
Desperate raging, wounded animal, scowls,
Hard to be deaf, to ignore those howls.

Wounds, once septic and raw
Became protected behind my wall.
Time heals – or so they say
The scars I bear just the price to pay.

My wall I removed some time ago
Jesus the true healer loves me so.
My hope no longer lies with man
My life to follow God's wonderous plan.

A MOMENT

Lois Houghton

A glance across a crowded platform
green eyes meet for a moment.
She smiles.
Time stops, his mouth dry
his future in her eyes
her soft breath on his neck
carrying his name, sweetly.
Tangled sheets, binding them together,
they are dancing, she is laughing,
they are one.
She turns, steps on the train,
the doors close, it pulls away.
In a moment
what a life
what a love that could have been.

HOMELESS IN OXFORD

Donna Macaulay

The sleeping bag crumpled,
Bare, nylon threads stubble,
His face waxy, blue sheened.
Hard to fathom where he lies.
An obelisk his pillow,
Ornately, sculpted for
Some privileged past grief.
His mattress of grass and soil,
Coffin sprung, to support firmly.
No fear, as he is half dead,
Alcohol soaked, drug lifted,
Shuffling out of life, it seems.
People tread the pavements,
Purposeful, endless chat, strut,
Motor the roads, horns honking.
Children bounce wildly on toes,
The happiest rubber balls.
He lies, blanket to rough chin,
His life trail unknown, dangling.
Newspaper, wedging the stone.
On the dense mat of his hair.

THE THIEF

Lois Houghton

His kisses should be sweet
it's what she needs
he bites her lip
it bleeds.
The soft caress
of fingers on her neck
tighten
as he steals her breath away.
The beauty he makes her feel is real
but he taunts, he steals
he shines his light on her.

And she glows, for a while.

He snuffs it out
takes her smile
and when the salt of her tears
is all that's left.
He is gone.
She is stolen.

IN TIME FLOWERS CAN BLOOM REGARDLESS

Will Mackenzie

I am afraid, trembling with the horrors of the universe.
Monsters beat on my door
or is that my heart I hear?

Time crawls.
It drags.
Seconds like talons through my mind.
I can feel it hanging over me, a creature I cannot see
but which knows my every move and thought.
Am I prey to be devoured?

It smells my blood as it pulses through my veins.
My body tenses
I wait for the bite but the teeth never come.
It chooses torment over the kill.

Darkness is the easy part: now here comes the light.
I open the door,
slip into the world with all its hidden dangers.
Along the pavement, my gaze low,
safe from inquisitive looks
or interactions fraught with uncertainty.

Distracted by the small spring buds at the edge of the
road,
not knowing their names nor they mine,

but I see their beauty and share the fragility.
Delicately, they peer from the safety of the side,
careful not to be trodden.
The breeze is still cold, but I can feel the season changing,
realise that in time,
flowers can bloom regardless.

Then, one morning a moment of clarity
I see the demon that stalks me
It looks strangely familiar as it stares deep into my soul.
Run or fight?

The season changes,
flowers can bloom regardless.

I stare back at it, deep into my reflection,
slowly it backs down, retreating into my shadow,
identity exposed and weakened.
I know it will never leave, so we'll share this space,
accepting each other like wolves in the pack.
Always by my side but alpha no more.

MEMORIES OF A CROFT

Glenise Borthwick

To touch the wood where wool was spun,
To spin the wheel and recall vivid memories
Of the clattering pedal and the woven basket filling up
With strands of wool that would transform into
pullovers,
Neither appreciated nor comfortable.

To look into boxes with remnants of a way of life,
Rusted and broken pieces that are a jigsaw of my being.
Oil lamps and cooking pots once loved and relevant,
Now kept as a connection to a way of life
Fading and receding.

Still hanging in the barn on rusting hooks are precious
finds
From over forty years ago.
Green glass fishing weights, coloured ropes, shells and
Viking buckles
Lost and found on a Scottish beach,
Now just fingerprints of other lives.

Rising out of the earth with every spade, whilst cutting
into the peat,
Come relics of former activities.

A ceramic jam jar, shards of colourful blue china, a watch
long rusted.
One old boot, with rusted nails clinging to a worn leather
sole.
A crofting way of life in miniature.

Paths long abandoned, fields bordered by fences held
together with rusting wire,
And tufts of fleece torn from passing sheep long gone.
In the wind memories of songs sung by birds and
ancestors
Accompanied by the howling and the whistling of the
ancient pine trees.
Sights and sounds calling out connecting past and present.

Smells of the burning peat, pungent and intense
A product of long hours of toil with
Cutting and drying just for a moment of warmth.
A moment laced with thoughts of cold days and long
nights
With the sod sparking and mesmerising.

Easy, often too easy, to remember those years
And a sentimental connection with a small croft
That has eased its way down a line of feisty, vibrant
woman
Who crofted and fought the elements, and now lie two
miles away
In the unbearable quiet of the local graveyard.

The responsibility of this small croft now lying with the
last in the line
Disconnected from both culture and traditions.
Left fearful for not being part of a legacy hard fought for.

Unable to speak the poetry of Gaelic ancestors and now
Left to apologise to those long gone in a much less lyrical voice.

Yet the land endures and the sounds, sights and scents repeat each day
Creating a thread that weaves into a new pattern, a new way of life.
Not so much a loss but a transformation with the land bending and changing
To meet the needs of a new generation.
Past and present intertwining in the very fibre of a tortured soul unable to let go.

SHE THE SEA

Lois Houghton

She calls me
Draws me in
Rhythmically
In, Out
In, Out
Shifting pebbles
She's cold
She, the sea
She takes my breath away
She spits it back, salty
In time with hers
In, Out
In, Out
She steals my thoughts
Empties my mind
Relax
And breathe
In, Out
In, Out
She's cold
She warms my soul
She spits me out
Whole
She, the sea

STAC POLLAIDH

Sam Phipps

jagged crown
crumbles
across millennia
loch liquefies sky
our breath
touches this land

THE CRAW DEIL

Lois Houghton

Waving away craws with someone else's tattered hands
scattering the blackest hearts
across wheat, across barley
in a borrowed coat that wears the stains of another life.
The dram spilt, the smoke breathed out
in the telling of exaggerated tales,
stories woven through its tweed.
The small bone button in the torn pocket
she said she'd sew it on –
a promise broken, long forgotten.
Ragged fabric
Flapping in the wind
Dancing
As it had burled and spun around the dance floor with the
button girl
whirling like the birds as they scatter on the wing.

THE STREAM MEETS THE RIVER

Neil Keay

It's raining
The hilltop rock pool fills
Overflowing
Trickling at first
Following the beaten path
Hewn out by years
Snaking and writhing
Like some demented creature
Picking up speed and body
As the gradient steepens
Cascading over rocks, squeezing through the gaps
Hurrying now
Ever quicker as the rain intensifies
Escaping the confines of its track
The flowing water amplified
A muted roar takes over
Faster, faster
Now rushing down the hill
On towards the river
Which Crashes and booms across its path
Snarling
Gnashing
A rabid monster
Out of control
It reaches out and consumes the stream

With overwhelming power
Nature's watery predator
What once was there
Is, in an instant
Gone.

PEBBLE

Sam Phipps

teased and tugged
I go where I go
wherever weight shape
size tides move me

I am of the sea
I am of the land
I am of the air

sometimes I sense the dent
of sand sometimes I twist
or flip I am born to this spin
this whoosh clatter kiss

I am of the sea
I am of the land
I am of the air

I will be smoothed to nothing
the nothing will not be nothing
maybe a trillion particles
of something

I am of the sea
I am of the land
I am of the air

Poetry

HAREBELLS

Donna Macaulay

The harebells are ringing, their sapphire hues.
Drawing the eye to enchanted thimbles,
Clustered petals of cerulean blues,
Where my cold finger longingly lingers.

Robust, in clamour of wildflower meadow,
Squeezing from crumblings of dry stone wall,
The tangle and clog of verge and hedgerow
Or pinched crevice, scoured from gritty cliff fall.

Miniature belfries of miracle and healing,
Toll softly to soothe the pain of passing.
Swelling to courage, the slumps of feeling,
Knotted in gut, seeming everlasting.

Chimes resilient in the summer breeze,
Pealing mighty consolations, to ease.

NOT TODAY

Anthony S. Holroyd

I have felt the gaping maw of death
Yawning expectantly beneath.
Gullet open, dark and wide,
Waiting for me to fall
Into his outstretched jaws.

On the wrong side
of a mountain ridge
I lost the path.
Beneath me only rocks and snow
A thousand foot or more below.

Crampons and axe pick
Doggedly bit
All that was keeping me from falling.
Slowly, I levered my anchor free
Reached above and plunged it deep

Four times I knocked on the door of fate
Until it held and took my weight
Anchored in the mountains side.
And slowly, inch by inch, I kicked my toes –
Stinging steps into the snow.

And in this fashion –
By careful, painful action

I inched up the ridge.
Until at last the top was gained –
I crawled on my belly, like a babe.

I know I will meet again with death
In the days or weeks or years ahead.
And I will look him in the eye, defiantly
As I enter his embrace
But not on that mountain and not in this way
Not today death
Not today.

THE BUBBLE

Will Mackenzie

Seemingly from nowhere,
a life so fragile.

Delicate

Valuable as any,
from the moment of conception.

Life,
from the breath of another

Beauty,
comparable to none.
Swirling rainbows of colour
on the sea of an unknown world.

As if with ease,
You rise,
You fall,
Navigating hedges and trees.

Guided by some magical hand,
hesitating for a moment,
as if to acknowledge my watching.

I know you fear every thorn,

just as I.
So I wish you well
on your perilous journey.

As time goes by,
every second we age,
our skins becomes thinner,
then
no more.

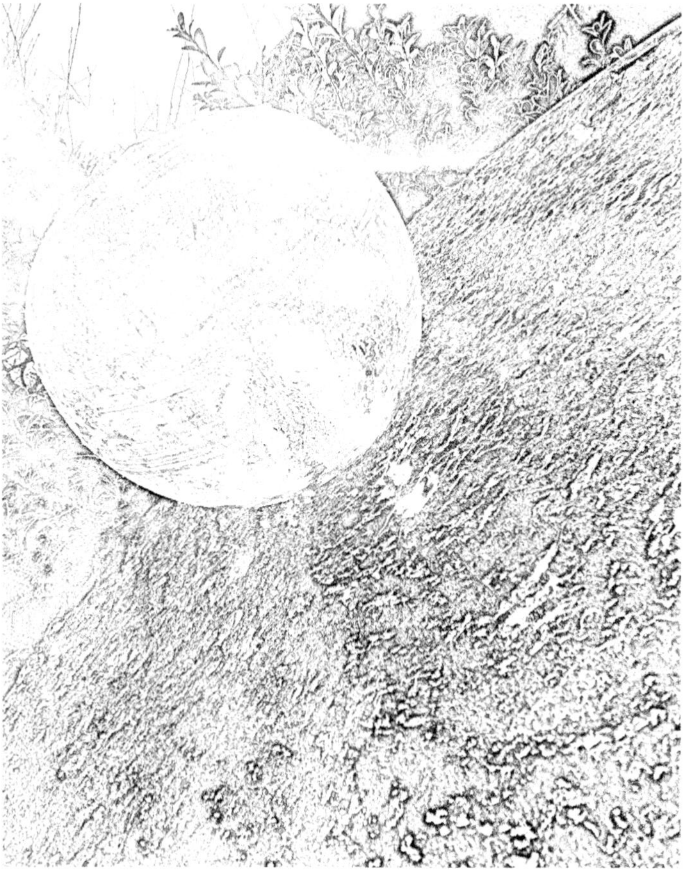

ODE TO COVID

Neil Keay

I'm sitting here in quarantine
Reflecting on the past few days
Where have I gone, who have I seen
To catch this bug, Covid nineteen.
It started with a wee sore throat
And then a shiver, get my coat
The headache built to join the rest
It's time to do a short flow test
With bated breath I watch the chart
Trepidation in my heart
One mark appears, it could be fine
But no, alas, that second line
Within the front room who can say
How long before I'm out to play
Just grin and bear it until then
In the doghouse once again.

BAD POEM

Andrea Pearson

Bad poems come easy to me.
I can choose some words and stick them together
In a nice easy rhythm, I can go on forever.
Bad poems come easy to me.

Lazy metaphors come easy to me.
Down the rivers of my brain they flow
And waterfall onto the page below.
Yes, lazy metaphors come easy to me.

A weak simile? I have one of those.
Sickly sweet as a sugar paste rose.
My imagery outta not be dull as dishwater
But it's just the way of it I s'pose.

It's no fault of our tutor who's done all she can do
To find a depth of emotion and a voice that is true.
But it's just a lost cause – come, take a look,
This bad poem will never appear in a book.

THE WORLD AROUND US

PAISLEY PATTERN

Andrea Pearson

What is this pattern?
What do you see?
A mango fruit
In a sunlit tree?

A shimmering jewel
In a Mughal hoard?
A pinecone, bloodied
By a crusader's sword?

A Kashmiri rose
Fragrant and sweet
Stolen from a father
Numbed by defeat?

The sweat of the enslaved
Bent over cotton
Where indigenous people
Are long since forgotten?

The tears of the weavers
At click-clackety looms,
Their shuttles frantic
As the world consumes?

Or a flickering flame

In the rising heat
Of a simmering world
While the pattern repeats?

Do you see it now?
How it begs us to stop.
Blood, sweat and grief,
The world in a teardrop.

BUT WHAT NEXT?

Claire Harris

Frequently we hear of migrants rescued from unsafe vessels attempting to cross the Channel. They arrive, full of relief that their journey is over. They've finally reached a place safe from war, violence, discrimination. But are they really? What happens after the elation of the first couple of days when the realisation of the next few years is upon them?

I saw a picture of a family this week. They'd been picked up by a lifeboat and offloaded at Dungeness. I remember Dungeness from my childhood. My grandparents lived up the coast, and I recall being taken for a pub lunch around there. The beach was full of perfectly round, sandy-coloured pebbles, almost like eggs. Once, I found a sun-bleached branch of driftwood while I was walking, and I remember being fascinated by its colour. It looked like nothing I'd ever seen before. The pub had big windows that looked over the expansive beach towards the power station. It seemed a vast distance away, but I expect it was just because I was small. We used to have chicken in a basket and possibly even a carvery. I can't really remember. No vegetables, of course.

The father envelops his three boys, all under the age of seven. They're from Syria, the caption says. His head is bowed, and I can't see his face. The eldest is almost entirely enfolded in his body, caught between his father's arms and the backs of his brothers. Only he and his youngest brother look directly at me. His face shows a self-conscious half grin, like he's been told he should always smile for the camera. The youngest, standing in front of him, looks ahead too, his face full of questioning incomprehension. The middle brother has the same look. The same turn in the lips and question in his eyes. He is the only one looking elsewhere. Back to the lifeboat, perhaps? Watching to see who else is arriving? Or looking back further perhaps their way of life, his family, his friends? Where is their mother, I wonder.

It's a beautiful day – the photo was taken in August, but where do they go next? Do they end up in some grimy, grey, Holiday Inn in Glasgow City Centre? Unable to work, having to make do with whatever faceless bureaucrats decide is best. Eating the slush provided, living in a country where we delude ourselves we're welcoming to immigrants. We like to think we're open-minded and easy-going, but we're not. "Migrants welcome" means not right this bit where I am, somewhere else please.

So yes, I wonder what happens next.

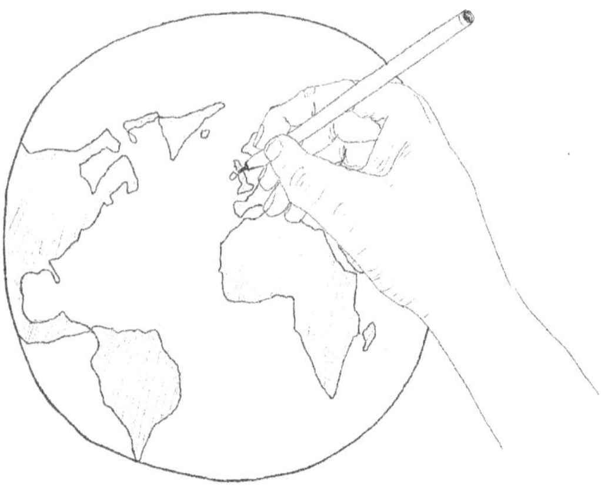

DEATH BY WATER

Anthony S. Holroyd

This is a response to the image of Alan Kurdi, 3 years old, drowned and washed ashore in Turkey whilst fleeing with his family from Syria.

The sea has an endless capacity to love. Everything we reject will be embraced by Poseidon. Alan – like so much flotsam – lost and claimed. Our conscience is jetsam, we abandon it to lighten the load – we tell ourselves it is the only way we can stay afloat. "Look after our own". *Nostrum genus primum.* We have enough problems at home. Who can love the stranger when our family is cold and hungry? Who can love a person they do not see? Poseidon will. What we reject is always claimed by the sea.

But Poseidon's love is so boundless that he gave his newly begotten son to us, washed on that beach. Face down… The sleep of babes. Peaceful, untroubled by our sins – by waves and currents; by bombs and bullets; the howls of mourning and of hatred; the shrugs of apathy. He slept untroubled, like the Phoenician. His body returned to us but unrisen. Sea water and silt still in his lungs. Claimed, embraced, and loved by Poseidon – a benevolent god showing us our folly. One who loves where we did not.

O you who turns from suffering when it is not of your blood or creed:

Phlebas was once as tall as you – consider Alan, who never will be.

SUCH AN AFTERNOON

Keith Davidson

As an exercise in perspective, our Creative Writing For Wellbeing class was asked to consider a subject that made us all feel squeamish: the point of view of Nazis murdering Jews during World War Two. The brief, in outline, was to write as a Nazi officer who had taken pity on his personal slave, a Jewish woman. When the time came, he decided to execute her quickly rather than see her suffer – his version of compassion. What I wrote was not poetry, nor even prose. It was a monologue from a film scene, telling only a very small part of a bigger story.

(Camera focuses on a close shot of a pair of hands, clasped together on a desk. We can't see the speaker (male), nor anyone else in the vicinity, just his hands on the desk. The accent is German but the language is English. As he talks, his hands move in synch with his words. The camera stays tight on his hands.)

"My uncle lived in Potsdam. We visited him on the first Sunday of the month when I was a child. Every month. My mother and father gathered my younger brothers and I together and we drove across the city to the main train station. Do you know Potsdam? It was a short trip; twenty minutes, maybe twenty-five.

Uncle always had cake ready for us, and some chocolate when he could afford it. He lived next to Babelsberg Park. He was a carpenter; aunt had died during the war.

The house was modest, but the garden was pleasant. Uncle took very good care of the garden. From the back door, it was twenty metres to a wooden fence. The park was on the other side.

When I was very small, he would sometimes call the foxes. Some food in a saucer, on a wooden board a few steps from the back door, and they would come. The foxes had made a hole under the wooden fence. Their homes were in the park but also they came to the houses and looked for pieces of food. My uncle was not the only one who gave them food.

The foxes were handsome. The fur was red and thick, faces suspicious, but when you saw their eyes, you wondered what they saw. The foxes gave me joy. Cakes and foxes and my nice uncle. The family trips to Potsdam are good memories. What an adventure at this age.

I got older; there were fewer trips. Also, my uncle was getting older and my parents were busy. I had more thoughts for friends, girls, school. But I remember the last occasion I was in Potsdam. My mother asked me to go to my uncle. Only me. I didn't ask why. I was fifteen, perhaps? It was not even a Sunday. I took the train from the main station and I was very happy to travel for the first time, alone.

Uncle had cake and even coffee. He knew that I was growing up. He said something about a small glass of cherry brandy but told me that mother would not forgive him. We laughed. Then he asked me to go out the back door with him.

He placed a saucer of food on a wooden board, close to the back door, like when I was very small. A vixen came. She was in good condition: a good size and bright eyes. When she ate the food, uncle reached into his coat.

He had a revolver from the war. He loaded it, and shot her. Then shot her again.

I shook. The noise of the revolver, the smell of it. Death. It was not expected on such an afternoon. I did not know what to say or do. I was fifteen. Uncle turned to me. He said I must always remember that vermin are vermin, even when they are beautiful. They have no place in our world."

WRITTEN ON THEIR HANDS

Catriona Henderson

Stars, eyes and random symbols. My children adorn their hands and arms with felt pen and biro drawings, decorating knuckles and fingernails. Like henna, these fade over time and are quickly replaced. Still too young to use their skin to record reminders or other seemingly vital prompts, they delight in their increasingly ornate self-defacement. It is an act of defiance by children whose privileged lives mean their main complaint in life is having to wash more often than they want to.

Having agreed that permanent pens are not to be used on skin, weekly swimming classes and showers after the other sports they do mean that it's rare for drawings to survive more than a week. Beyond a passing interest in the most visible of their artwork, I have little concern for whether a particular picture or pattern lasts or doesn't. The most danger they are in is from chemicals in the ink seeping through their skin, and I choose to ignore this.

Two and half thousand miles away, the writing on other children's hands is a much more serious matter. Names are written so that children can be identified if they are pulled from rubble. If they are alive, they can be reunited with any family members who have survived the blast.

If they are dead, they can be more easily identified.

We cried when we heard about this in the news, our impotent tears a searing reminder of the inequity between the lives of our children and those living in constant terror. With mounting deaths and over a million displaced, the numbers become increasingly difficult to comprehend. As the situation worsens, it is harder to grasp and easier to switch off. But imagine that you have no way of knowing if you or your children will be alive tomorrow, and that there is nothing you can do but wait and hope. Imagine writing your child's name on their hands or arms in case you are all blown up. Imagine this being the only real action you can take to try to make sure your child can be identified. Imagine.

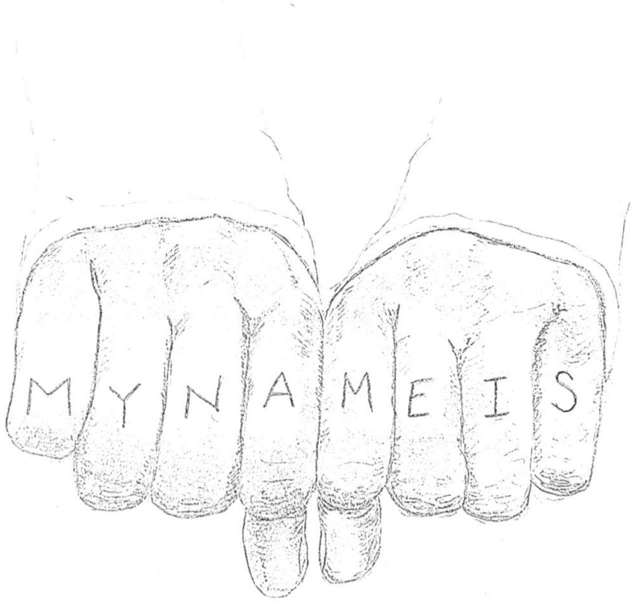

With virtually no water to drink or to cook with, there is no chance those names will be washed off. Swimming in the sea, previously a welcome relief from the crammed space bound on three sides by hard land borders through which most people are forbidden to pass, is the last thing on anyone's mind. Instead, all energy is put into much more basic and urgent things. Where will they find water? Food? Medicines? Shelter? Safety? Even a pen? Whether the pens are permanent or not is the least of their concerns. Surviving for another day is an achievement in itself.

My children hate washing. It's an ongoing battle to get them into the shower when they come home tired and muddy from football training on a waterlogged playing field, or sweaty from judo. Along with a general aversion to water unless it's the sea or a swimming pool, they are indignant that their hands and arms emerge from showers as clean canvases, their latest artistic efforts rinsed down the drain. As they emerge, vaguely clean and very grumpy, it's never long until they take up their pens again. It's hard not to wonder how many children's lives will be erased before my children's latest drawings, and how many of those will only be identifiable by the names written on their hands.

ANORAK

Keith Davidson

You don't expect the Lord to appear unto you anywhere really, least of all at the beach links down in Banff. I was walking back towards Banff itself when this woman coming the other way said, "See anything good?"

I forgot that I had a pair of binoculars slung round my neck, intent on bird species that lived behind the foreshore. I had clocked two blackbirds and nothing else.

"Blackbirds," I said. "But there were all kinds of seabirds that way earlier," and I nodded in the direction I was heading.

"I like blackbirds, though," she said. Then she kept on talking.

If she hadn't told me I would have guessed early sixties; she wore a very colourful anorak that looked as if it was made from a vinyl tablecloth; there were two dogs at her heels. I checked them out later on the internet and made a wild guess that they were so bespoke no one had come up with a breed name for them yet, hyphenated or otherwise.

As the dogs were fussing around my feet I asked what she called them.

"Metatron and Uriel," she said.

Seeing the surprise on my face she smiled and added, "No, not really. They're called Tootsie and Coco."

She didn't quite give me her life story but she did say she was on holiday for a week which seemed fairly unlikely in Banff in early November; that herself and her husband Alistair had rented a cottage; that she just loved the foreshore, the sea air and how it blew the cobwebs from her head.

She asked what I was doing there. I mentioned an elderly father in a wheelchair and months of hospitalisation. In return, she talked about her mother who had been carried away in her late eighties on waves of cellulitis and septicaemia. After we parted, I had to look up cellulitis on the internet on my phone, as well the dogs thing.

At this point, as we stood chatting about the relaxing features of birdwatching among other matters, I wasn't aware that she was the Lord, or that the dogs really were Metatron and Uriel who were under deep, and very effective, cover. You don't really expect God to have a pensioner's bus pass – she told me about that too – or a husband called Alistair. Or that God would have had a nervous breakdown at some point in her life – if life is the kind of concept that can be applied to God. But she told me about the breakdown, inevitably, and how birdwatching had helped, even though birdsong in the mornings had initially driven her even further out of her tree than she had been already.

For an unexpected chat, sharing the human moment – talking about curlews, bereavement, septicaemia and family – it was comforting. She even touched me on the arm, in a supportive way. Friends hardly do this in Banff, let alone strangers.

But despite all that – the chat, the personal revelations, the shared interest, the adventurous anorak – I had no idea I was talking to the Lord. The Lady? Gender roles are deeply embedded in the language we speak and think with, aren't they? Anyway, I had no idea I was talking to God until she touched me on the arm for a second time and said, "I'll let you get on."

She walked by me, going in the opposite direction as per when we started the conversation, and I spun around to say, "Enjoy the rest of your holiday," as a suitably polite conclusion.

But she had gone. Instead of pensioner-bus-pass-lady and two wee dogs there was a goldfinch, head cocked, standing on the path, flanked by the angel of repentance and the chancellor of heaven. It was pretty impressive – even the herring gulls looked worried. Then the goldfinch flew away, darting, quickly, and the angels receded. I know receded sounds a bit weird but it's the best I can come up with.

Back at dad's house I had a look at the RSPB Handbook Of British Birds, page 283: the goldfinch. Exactly the same colours as that anorak.

MAKING A DIFFERENCE

Neil Keay

My name is Mohammed. Born and raised in Karachi, Pakistan, to parents Inaya and Hassan, 32 years ago. I attended Karachi Grammar School and, after obtaining my higher qualifications, secured a place in the University of Karachi studying medicine. As my father is a GP and my mother a senior nurse in Patel hospital, I suppose it was inevitable that I would follow them into the medical profession. My wish is to become a surgeon and that is my goal. Over the next four years I studied hard and, at the end of it, passed all disciplines with distinction.

After leaving university I applied for, and was fortunate enough to be granted, a post as a junior doctor with Patel Hospital. On completion of my studies, I began training as a surgeon at the same hospital in my home city. I worked alongside my mother gaining a wealth of experience as years went on. Eventually, to my family's delight – and my own – I received promotion to surgeon, my goal. I was very proud and immensely satisfied knowing that, by saving lives, I was making a difference.

Every day I pray to God, thanking him for bestowing this gift upon me. I will use it wisely.

One evening, while watching the TV news about the horrors taking place in Afghanistan and the overwhelming loss of life in the war zone, particularly involving children, I became distraught. How could people do this to each other? The images were graphic. You see I, like many of my faith, was brought up to believe people and lives are precious and that we are put on earth to help one another. After hearing that there was a chronic shortage of doctors, my mind was made up. I needed to go there to help these poor people.

The paperwork needed to transfer countries went through easily and I made several phone calls to the local hospital there to arrange accommodation and work placements. I was determined, in my mind, to make a difference.

Within a few weeks of making enquiries, I had arrived in the war zone of Afghanistan. The taxi was waiting to take me to the hospital. I was met by the scene of pure desolation, destruction and devastation in what once, I believe, would have been a busy thriving city. There was barely a piece of ground that had no bricks or salvage, a result of continuous mortar fire, destroying houses and buildings. Craters, rubble and dust were all that was left behind.

Children were shoeless and crying, wearing dirty rags, their faces etched with sorrow and starvation. A few had the energy to come closer to the car and tap on the windows wailing, arms and hands stretched out wide, hoping we had food or water for them. These people had nowhere to go. Mothers cradling their young, crying out, begging through tears, despair all too evident on their weathered faces, lining the temporary home-made roadway to the hospital. Makeshift tents scattered around giving the only shelter they had from the hot sun.

I arrived at the hospital visibly shaken, and was shown to the converted ward that had been hastily turned into lodgings for six of us. I was shown round the ward where I was assigned to, and introduced to, the team I'd be working with. There was no time for real formalities as there was almost a conveyor belt of injured, sick and malnourished children to attend to. Time to get my doctor's PPE on and get to work, more determined than ever to make a difference.

The hospital itself was a scene of carnage with children of all ages spilling out into the corridors, some with parents, most with no-one, all waiting to be treated. The extent of the suffering and the severity of their injuries and general ill health was horrific. The task ahead of us was mammoth but I refused to believe insurmountable. We waded through the sea of people, highlighting the ones needing the most urgent care first. Many of the children suffered badly with malnutrition or diseases with the lack of clean water or food. A lack of beds meant operating sometimes on makeshift tables using standard lighting for illumination. We had to work in the corridors as darkness descended. Because this was a hospital, running water had been prioritised, backed up with water bowsers supplied by foreign aid. Food has also been made available, albeit in limited choice and quantities.

I worked for hours late into the night, with no respite except for the occasional comfort break. One of my colleagues, a doctor from Afghanistan who has been here since the beginning of the troubles, started the ghoulish practice of keeping a daily 'score' of patient mortality. Today it read... **SAVED 85 LOST 142.**

I was repulsed by this and asked him why he did it. He looked at me through world weary eyes as he replied, "It encourages us to do better tomorrow."

Around midnight, my relief came in to take over and as I walked to my place of rest, my eyes scanned the corridors and other wards. There seemed to be just as many casualties as before. My thoughts turned to grief then despair. Had I done enough to try to save those who died at my hands? Sitting on my bed in this converted ward gave me time to survey my surroundings. Not many creature comforts here. A bed, lockers, shower room, toilet, washbasin and phone charging point all shared between six of us. Looking at the rest of the team, they all seemed the same as me: exhausted, dejected and realising the magnitude of our task.

I prayed again, asking for the strength needed to cope with what lay ahead.

The picture of my doctor colleague's 'scorecard' which had at first repulsed me, shone clearly in my mind. The more I thought about it the more, in a macabre way, it made sense. We needed to feel that we were making a difference and if we could see less kids dying and more living through our efforts, it would give us the strength to go on.

As the days dragged into weeks, it became harder for us to remain upbeat. There seemed no end to the sick and dying coming through those doors. The hardest part of it all was watching the children we knew could be saved, needlessly dying because we didn't have the drugs or medicines available, to at least ease their suffering.

We are all exhausted now and despondent. Morale is very low, due to the critical lack of medicines, and the rising mortality rate.

The "scorecard" seems to be becoming more and more important to me as I find myself referring to it first thing in the morning and constantly throughout the day, almost like a timepiece. A mortality watch.

I am a deeply religious man but find myself questioning my beliefs and even beginning to ask myself if there is a God.

I pray every night but find my prayer time shortening. I ask why a caring God, one I revere, has forsaken those innocent children? I await a reply.

A foreign correspondent from a British news channel came to the hospital one day, making a video report of the current situation. I explained what we did, adding that the number of children dying now topped two hundred per day. We tried to do the best we could within the restraints given to us. He looked distressed. After filming was finished, I heard from a colleague that he (the reporter) had run, ashen faced, to the bathroom where he threw up.

Every day was the same. We couldn't go outside because it's too dangerous, so we just carried on with 'our lot' saving who we can, trying to make a difference, although I sometimes wondered if I was.

I awoke one morning to the sound of cheering from some quarters of the hospital, prompting me to quickly get out of bed, get dressed and, together with my colleagues, rush through to the source of the commotion. It seemed the war was finally over, and the ceasefire negotiations were underway.

I prayed again, but this time it was tinged with a sense of shame on my part. My God had stopped the war. I had let my frustrations and my empathy for the children's suffering shake my faith. Who was I to question this higher power? I begged forgiveness.

The mood throughout the hospital brightened as word spread.

As the days unfolded, we attended to our tasks with renewed vigour, and a sense of cautious optimism filled the air. News filtered through about the imminent withdrawal of the liberating forces returning to their own countries, the Afghan government deemed structured enough to control its own affairs.

I prayed to God, thanking him for ending the bloodshed.

At the start of each day, our first port of call was always our beloved scorecard. Sure enough, the death toll began to drop, but not by as much as we had hoped. On further investigation we found, to our dismay, that the precious medical supplies required were not arriving in nearly the quantities promised.

Our concerns were raised with the hospital governors and local authorities, who promised answers.

At this time, I had received a text from my parents in Pakistan, informing me that a position of senior surgeon had become available at Patel hospital. Apparently, the hospital board had been monitoring my work out here and were greatly impressed, and would be keen to offer me this position. As my work permit was nearing its renewal date, this made the offer doubly tempting. But what of the children?

I was torn. Should I pass up the chance of a lifetime, or stay here and try to make a difference? I deliberated over my dilemma for two days until fate made my mind up for me.

The scorecard had almost flattened off, showing no appreciable drop in the mortality rate. The medical supplies were still well short of quota, while the percentage of malnourished and dehydrated children seemed worryingly constant.

At last, the hospital governors called us in for a meeting. They had our answers. Not the ones we wanted to hear. The supplies we ordered were dispatched but, due to the increasing guerrilla activity, the convoys were being hijacked and the contents sold on the black market.

Likewise, food and clothing didn't seem to be getting to where they were needed. Corruption is everywhere.

During my daily prayers, it became increasingly clear to me that lawlessness and greed were becoming more commonplace. My God had done all he could but, as seems to be the case, whenever there is war and suffering, certain people try to profit from misery. A power struggle with the innocents as pawns. The fault is not God's, but man's.

I've had enough of the inhumanity here!

I texted the board at Patel hospital thanking them for the offer of employment which I would be honoured to accept, stating that, as soon as I could arrange return travel and tie things up here, I would arrange to meet with them. I then texted my parents with my decision. They replied informing me that they would arrange flight tickets home for me.

After informing the authorities of my decision to return home, I faced the painful task of telling my colleagues, some of whom had become close friends. We have come through so much together. I feel that I'm letting them down. Thankfully, they all seemed to understand my reasons. I'd like to have had more time to thank everyone individually, but no time. My last day at work beckoned.

The next day was the flight home. Transport had been arranged to take me to the airport. Before leaving, I couldn't help but have one last look at that scorecard. No real change in the statistics. This saddened me. The memory of this will live with me forever.

After out goodbyes, my transport took me to the airport along the same route as when I arrived. Looking out of the window, there seemed no differences now to when I had seen the carnage in what seemed like an eternity ago. Starving children wearing the same rags as before. Hopelessness etched on the faces of their parents. Desolation. Where was their brave new world? What was the point of it all?

I arrived at the airport and checked in. My tickets were waiting for me. I boarded the plane in a sombre mood.

As we took off, the faces of the people I had seen burned into my mind.

The war may be over, I mused, but for the Afghan people, their fight has just begun.

VACCINATION LIES

Catriona Henderson

So here we are, just the two of us for the very last time. Hardly a romantic setting among these beeping, wheezing machines that are keeping you alive. I hate them almost as much as I hate you. I'm not sure if you can hear me. Part of me hopes you can, though the part of me that still feels the ghost of the love I thought was real wishes that you are past that given what I want to say. Hardly a fond farewell.

Not that there have been many kind words between us recently. I really thought all the arguments had been worth it in the end, when you finally conceded that other people were more important than your conspiracy theory-fuelled anti-vax posturing.

"People aren't dying from it," you said.

And what I saw of the exhausted and despairing medics I served in the canteen three floors below the covid wards was dismissed as propaganda and exaggeration. The same went for the death toll racking up, each addition leaving behind a bereaved family, though in the early days they had no option of vaccinations to give them and their families the best possible chance. Not like us. By the time you were brought here, you were probably past being able to see the hollowness in the doctors' faces for yourself, though by then it was far too late anyway. Already you were destined to be one of the statistics, soon to become another story in a local paper about a life lost too early, accompanied by the obligatory smiling photos of our wedding. I can already feel the burning humiliation of the hypocrisy, starting in my heart and extending its creeping fingers of shame until it has engulfed me from the inside. My reflex defence of curling into myself only takes me closer to my own degradation.

"What if it makes me infertile?"

What rubbish, but what if it had? We already have the kids we wanted, though they won't have a dad. You've wrenched that away from them. I haven't let them see me cry, as one of us has to be strong enough to at least pretend that we have a future to look forward to, though I have no idea what that will be. But any strength I have is an illusion I am only just managing to project to the outside world, while inside I feel disorientated and shattered. The whole world is spinning at divergent speeds. Things suddenly loom into focus highlighting what I have lost or am about to lose my grip on, before blurring into a haze of pain and grief and disbelief.

It takes all my concentration just to stay upright as the dizziness whips my bearings from me and untethers my mind. Sitting here, it appears I am barely moving, yet this is an illusion of stillness, as inside pandemonium is winning and there is no peace in my world. I am torn apart by resentment at the care you are getting, while I am the one left to pick up the pieces of everything you have shattered. I won't let you take away the children's last happy memories of you and replace it with this one of you, impotent and unmoving. They deserve better. So the kids haven't come to say goodbye and are at your sister's playing with their cousins, old enough to know what is happening but still young enough to have no idea what this will mean, and just how much harder life will be. Small mercies indeed.

"I work from home so I'm never going to pick it up," you said.

But with Daniella at nursery and Oliver at primary school, and me working at the hospital, you weren't living in a bubble other than the one in your own head. I tried so hard to keep us all safe, the constant handwashing and clothes washing and hand sanitizer and arguments from the kids about how much they hated the smell and the gloopiness on their small hands. We stopped going places that were busy, though I never told you how many invitations to play with other kids I took away from our two. There was enough resentment between us without putting the kids in the middle of it all, but they paid the price regardless. And we will all continue to pay the price. Forever. In ways I could never have imagined.

When I try to look beyond the next hour or two, I am engulfed by the enormity of the despair and desolation filling my whole horizon and beating back my attempts to find a point to focus on that might get us to a more stable place. Your firmly rooted belief that you were safe and clever and knew best has taken away the foundations of our lives, but you aren't going to be here to try to make sense of the rubble. Dying is by far the easier option, and I almost wish it were me who was about to leave all responsibility behind. You certainly deserve to be the one who has to deal with the devastation that is our future.

"I'm young and fit, it won't make me ill," you said.

Circumstances prove otherwise, and it may have been your trips to the gym that killed you, albeit by association with this evil virus than through the daily routine you imposed on yourself. I will never know which of us is culpable. I hope it's you, though there have also been moments when I have wished it was me, imagining that I am exacting revenge without you even knowing. Fitness and optimism, or maybe more stupidity and ignorance, have been no match for covid, and it would almost have been funny to see the confusion and disbelief on your face as you got more and more unwell, if the consequences weren't so savage for us all. Of course, I didn't think it would ever get to this stage because you had been vaccinated.

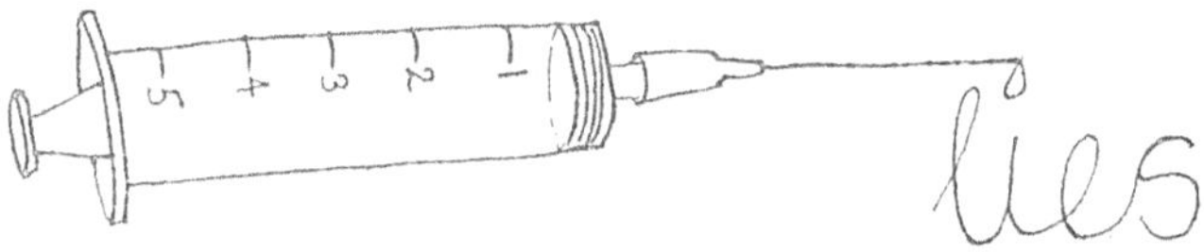

We exhausted ourselves with the same arguments until you finally said you would go. Said you agreed that it was important to make sure the kids and our parents were kept safe, and that it was no big deal and that no, you hadn't had many side effects beyond one day of feeling under the weather and a bit achy and having a sore arm. We stopped arguing about covid, the routines of rigid handwashing and me changing out of my work clothes in the garage and washing them separately to everything else were dropped. "It's been worth getting the jags just to stop all that bollocks," you said.

We also relaxed back into our usual arguments about how we were going to pay the bills. Couldn't I buy less expensive food, though anything beyond basics were already treats that were few and far between, and why did the kids need new clothes again? I have no idea how I am going to keep our home and feed and clothe the kids. Until last week I had no real idea just how much debt we had. By the time we bury you we might not even have a home to live in, and for that I hate you more than anything. Being selfish is one thing, but taking away everything our kids have known is something else entirely. I am glad you are about to die because if you lived I would want to kill you.

My fury is bigger than I am, and I am terrified that if I start to let it out it might consume the world and me and the kids along with it. Now it batters me on the inside trying to find a way to escape and show its true dimensions, and I am amazed that people can't see the physical impact – how can such a visceral feeling be invisible when it is pinballing around my body and punching to find a way out. It is taking so much of my energy to contain this monster. I have stopped sleeping in case relaxing even for a moment will open up the space it needs to seep out and I will never be able to cram it back inside again.

I'm expected to be grieving for you, but if the doctors weren't about to switch off these chattering machines I would do it myself. Because you lied. You never went to those vaccination appointments, so little wonder you didn't have any side effects. Though you lied about that too, saying your arm was sore both times, and even had a day in bed after the first one because you claimed you felt under the weather. I could almost see the point of lying to hide an infidelity, trading me in for someone less exhausted by life and lacking the caution with which I approached your enthusiasm for enjoying today without worrying about tomorrow. I feel almost as stupid as if you had been having an affair, looking after you the day you weren't well after your first vaccination because I was so relieved you had gone to get it done. This lie is at least as destructive as if you were being unfaithful, and you won't even be about to pay the price. I wish I had worried more, agreed to less, and wasn't about to fall such a long way.

The lie was bigger than that, though. You lied about us being the most important thing, about being here to see the kids grow up and to be here for me and to do everything you could to make our family happy. Lies, lies, lies.

When you were put on a ventilator, I asked how it was possible when you had been vaccinated. Why wasn't that keeping you safe? Why were you so ill? Why couldn't they make you well? Why, why, why? Even through the masks and visors I saw the nervous look between the two nurses who were moving you to intensive care.

I recognized the doctor who took me into a side room where there was a box of tissues on the small plastic table and explained that you hadn't turned up for either of your appointments. I had seen them sitting crying in the canteen, overcome by the futility of trying to save people who were beyond help while putting themselves and their families at risk. With a gentleness I will never again feel towards you, they sat with my disbelief and confusion, even though they had better things to be doing. Better things than looking after you.

But that was only the start of your deception, or more accurately the final blow. As it became obvious just how seriously ill you were and that you might never come home, I gathered what energy and focus I had from the brink of my despair and sat with them and all the information I could find about our finances. Piecing together the jigsaw from bills and bank statements and loan agreements, the gaping hole became more and more obvious, but still I had no idea what the missing pieces were and trustingly hung on to the edges of my knowledge believing there must be a simple explanation. There must, because the alternative was beyond my reach to hold along with everything else that I was frantically trying to catch as my life crumbled around me.

And then I found the fragments, one by one, in emails on your computer until together they became something so large, so beyond naming that I could feel them towering over me and casting their dark, chilling shadow. As a sense of its hugeness took shape I bit the inside of my cheeks so hard to stop the scream escaping and waking the kids and the whole world that they bled for hours. My tongue constantly explores the scars, the physical pain a reminder that I am still able to feel despite a part of me retreating to a numbness I amn't sure will ever thaw. They are the only things that feel permanent anymore.

Thousands and thousands of pounds borrowed, gambled and lost. I discovered my signature on loan agreements, at the same time as I discovered that forgery was a skill I never knew you had. So much to learn about you when you were already past speaking. Almost past breathing. My own breath choking in shock, plugging my throat as forcefully as half-swallowed food and strangling me as I started to understand the wide sweep of your deceit.

I trusted you because I didn't know there were reasons not to. But now I have no idea what is real and what isn't. Of course, I knew that we were stretching ourselves financially, and we had so many discussions and quarrels about whether we could, should buy the house. But I was swayed by your reasoning that it would give our kids a stable place to grow up, space to have fun and share with family and friends, everything you lacked as a child. And although I wanted to look for a better job, one that used the qualifications I had worked so hard to get, you were unmoving in your belief that one of us should be here for the kids. One of us needed to have a job that fitted round them. One of us didn't need to worry about the money. If only one of us had.

I am shamed by what I have given up, given in to, and the precarious position I have fated for myself and our children through my casual faith in you. Reproach for myself that makes me want to shrivel from the world and never have to face the consequences of your fraudulence, or see the humiliation our children will feel as everything they know is wrenched from them. But I don't have that luxury. You were wagering our future, using my name to borrow money to fund your gambling and camouflage your debt and moral corruption.

Of the dozens of loans you have taken out, only two have been sanctioned by my signature. We had countless hours of debate about each of these so you knew there was no chance at all that I would have agreed to the others. And so you took the pen out of my hands without my knowledge and signed for these debts in my name once your own borrowing had grown to a stage where no-one was going to lend you anything more. Even then you kept gambling, your losses consuming the money needed to pay the bills and the few debts I knew about.

If only they were all we owed. Only now am I realizing just how little I know, about you and how precariously our lives are balanced. The hole in the jigsaw has taken shape as a vast, monstrous void which we're teetering on the edge of, and for which I alone have been left responsible. I feel that I am peering over the edge of an abyss so immense I can't yet see the bottom, and even though the scale of what I have uncovered so far seems unfathomable, it appears there is more deception to excavate.

The truth exposed in your emails is that you were as successful at gambling as you have been at surviving covid. Your only tangible achievement a ridiculous prevailing belief that you were above the rules that apply to everyone else, that this could continue and no-one would find out. You chose to ignore reality even though it must have been obvious that you had gone too far to survive the maelstrom of your own creating. In doing so you have staked every part of our future, rolling the dice and losing each time until we have less than nothing. The true cost of your fraud and duplicity is beyond anything my imagination can conjure. The threats from loan sharks hold more fear and uncertainty than I have the ability to comprehend on top of everything else I am trying and failing to grasp. It's game over in every sense.

I want to shake you until the answers I need rattle out of your rasping lungs. What of our partnership? Doing things together, for each other? I wonder if you ever saw me as an equal. And what about the children and the security you dangled for them as a lure for those first two loans? Everything I have found answers some questions but poses more in their place. What else don't I know? How much of the picture I have of our lives is fake, photoshopped by your lies to include things I thought were ours but are just elaborate covers for debt, and airbrushed to include a happiness I now know was built on a mirage? Maybe you were having an affair and were trying to fund two parallel lives. It wouldn't surprise me. How dare you leave without at least telling me the truth.

So now do I become a liar, complicit in deceiving our children? Or do I tell them how you fabricated the illusion of your care for us? Instead of having the two injections that would mean we would all be at home together looking to the future, however complicated and painful I now know that might be, you lied and lied and lied. If you had been honest about even that, at least I wouldn't be the only one left holding all responsibility. And do I explain to them that you gambled with our lives, building layers of deceit to hide the swirling debt that I can only guess you hoped to silently service while I was kept in the dark? Risking everything and squandering our family's future. If you were well, I might never have found out what a lie our lives were and how little of what I thought was real truly existed. Maybe I should be grateful that your vaccination lies have unmasked you instead of living a life built on nothing but a sham, and have saved our children from your pathological falsity. But no-one is a winner here. Either way I lose, and so do they.

I can see the doctor coming for the last time. You have certainly had enough of everyone's time. Far, far more than you deserve. I hope this bed and all the machines and pipes and wires can help someone who has been prepared to help themselves, and who does believe the people they claim to love are worth more than the consequences of dogmatic idiocy and deceit. That their lives are too valuable to gamble with. Maybe one day I will start to forgive you, but I doubt it. That would take resources I no longer have, and I'd venture that I never will. For as far into the future as I can see every scrap of my energy will be demolished trying to rebuild our lives from the devastation you have bequeathed us. How I wish you had enough awareness to grasp the irony of my signature being used legitimately to bring your pathetic life to an end.

LOOK ME IN THE EYE

Tina Norris

This poem is a response to an exercise asking participants to use a photograph in a war zone, of an emaciated child in her mother's arms, as a prompt.

Look Me In The Eye

My weakness
is your weakness, your fault.
Your crime.

My future
of laughing and loving,
of hard work and wide reward,
ends here.

Your choices
sweep mine away
in clouds of dust and violence.
My light,
extinguished by your privilege.

All I have is the desperate love of my mother,

grieving me
even before my child's fighting heart
is beaten.

I wanted more.

PROSE

A FLOWER JUST GROWING WILD

Brian Devlin

When I was wee my dad told me that pigs could see the wind. I looked at him.

"Pigs can see the wind?"

"Yes."

"What colour is the wind?"

"It's sort of bluey-pink," he said. "Maybe some grey."

I told my pals at school the next day.

"Pigs can see the wind."

"Wha?"

"Pigs can see the wind. I'm telling ye."

"Away ye go."

"It's true. It's pink and grey and maybe a bit blue."

Momentarily I became famous. For half an hour, until the teacher heard the story. I went home, angry and as cross as a wee five-year-old Scottish boy could be. Enraged, I waited until my dad came in.

"You-told-me-that-pigs-could-see-the-wind-and-I-told-Mike-and-he told-Sheena-and-she-told-Linda-and-Linda-told-Jules-and-Una said that's rubbish and-then Maura asked what colour was it-and I said blue and green. Bernie said I made her want to throw up."

My dad knelt down and put his arms around me and held me until my wee boy rage dissolved into sobs and bubbles. I couldn't be angry at my dad. My dad loved me. He smelt so nice.

His piece-bag that he carried his sandwiches in was yellow and fibrous. I asked him what was inside. He showed me. The waxy 'plain loaf' wrapper that he'd had his corned beef sandwiches in was traced with brown sauce. The quarter whisky bottle for his milk. A roll of wire for tying steel bars together. A pen knife. A teaspoon. A packet of cigarettes—Embassy regal. A box of Bluebell matches and some old betting slips. My dad adored me. We never fully understood one another. We had little in common. He held me and he let me sob my anger away into his chest. He was warm. He embraced me and I clung onto him.

When you're wee you do that don't you? You become overwhelmed by things: insecurities, nightmares and embarrassments. You wonder about the shadows in your bedroom, by what lurks under your bed. Then you call out as you can hear the laughter of the grown-ups in the other room, the music from the record player, "Campbelltown Loch, I wish you were whisky, Campbelltown Loch, Och Aye. Campbelltown Loch, I wish you were whisky, I would drink you dryeee."

Then uncle Jamie starts. You can hear the legs of the chair creaking on the floor as he stands.

"Shhh. Shhh."

"Jamie's a lovely voice on him."

"Aye. Lovely voice. Same as his faither."

"Will ye shoosh Bessie!"

"*Alone a boy was standing, and when I askt him whyee. He turned to me, he could not see, and he began to cry, Oh I'ma nobody's child, a-no-o-body's chi-e-ld.*"

And you call out to your mum. Furious that you're in bed when everyone else is up and you're about to begin your negotiations for fair play. She comes and sits at the side of your bed and you mean to say, "I want to be up in there with the rest o' yis." But you end up singing, "Twinkle, twinkle little star, how I wonder what you are," into her shoulder. She's had a Babycham and she's smiling and her eyes are wet at the same time.

"Where did you learn that?"

"At skail".

"School, Brian."

"Aye. At school."

And she lies down beside you. And you coorie in. You sleep then.

CONNECTIONS

Glenise Borthwick

The key in my pocket felt smooth and comforting. I had turned it over and over again before taking it out nervously and placing it into the lock of the door. A door immediately familiar with its flaking paint and worn hinges, holding memories of many visits. It creaked and had some resistance as I pushed it open.

Inside there was an immediate smell of dried peat and kerosine. The house had been empty for over a year and windows and shelves had a thick, suffocating dust on them. Family members looked out at me from photo frames dulled with age that told the story of my youth.

The house of my childhood, always warm and inviting, was now empty and soulless.

I opened the shutters and the light streamed in opening up vistas from my past.

It remained as he had left it the night they took him away.

Coats still hung on the large brass peg on the front door. The heavy woollen coat he had insisted always had one more winter's worth in it, still worn and damaged just as he had become, hanging with its pockets full of bits of rope, old nails, small stones from the shoreline.

Everything in the house had a sense that, had he ever returned, it would spring back into life.

The worn and blackened boots neatly placed by the fireside, the tin cups beside the old gas cooker as if ready to warm his hands from the kettle still sitting on the rusted ring.

The sound of that kettle boiling and the metal cups clinking had become an anthem to my youth. Always there when I visited him, always welcoming me home.

His newspaper, now yellowed, lay by his favourite seat, a seat close to the fire but placed to make the most of the view from the window. As young children we knew never to sit there for fear of reprisal.

I had delayed coming back to the house, partly through work commitments, but mainly through the pain of coming to terms with my loss. It was time to face my demons and start to close up the house.

This initial visit would be to choose some items. Memories of times we spent together. An indulgent trip. I looked around and started to make my choices.

By the fire was a small piece of driftwood I had found many years ago. It reminded me of a small vessel, like one of the ships my grandfather had spent his years on. He had laughed when I took my treasure home, yet he kept it and cleaned it and turned it into a family heirloom.

Nervously, I sat in his chair, still smelling the tobacco that had permeated the fabric. Smoking was his ritual and often he would sit outside looking over to the loch, telling me stories of ancient people and heroic battles when I was much younger, puffing contentedly between the vivid characterisations of those he peppered his tales with. Then it caught my eye. A small wooden box, insignificant, yet I was drawn towards it.

I opened it and there lay his cap badge from the war, a war he was always reluctant to talk about. We had always respected his reticence to talk about his experiences and knew these memories were his alone. It had been treasured by him, so I placed it into my bag along with the driftwood.

The musty smell was becoming overpowering so I took a few moments outside in the damp air. I had stood there many times looking over at the loch. I knew every mood, every outline. I could close my eyes yet still see it vividly in my mind, so engrained it was in my memory. The silence this time shocked me.

I was brought back to the present by the piercing call of a kestrel as it hovered gently, but with intent, over the trees. I shuddered when I remembered that same call the day my grandfather's ambulance drove slowly down the single track road, away from his home and his life forever. The blackened windows on the vehicle were as dark as my own despair.

A sudden knocking on the window behind me jolted me back to the present. An old piece of rope with a piece of stag's horn had tapped the window, caught by the gentle breeze now stirring.

The horn had been there for as long as I could remember. My grandfather had cut pieces off with his hacksaw, carving them miraculously into small buttons; buttons he kept in a battered tobacco tin and showed proudly to anyone he had ensnared into one of his long conversations about his life.

I can still hear that file rasping on the horn as he continued with his craft, hoping to have a full set for his favourite tweed jacket. My pleas for a knife handle were always ignored. I had felt cheated, since I had found the horn, to be denied a trophy from it.

Just about everything he had worked on had been left as if he would come back and complete the job. He seldom did and the croft was littered with incomplete tasks. It showed elements of energy and reluctance in equal measures.

Back in the cottage I found the tin button box where it had always been. Rusted now and rough to my touch, yellowing and worn from constant use. I had never known him without it.

He had led a very ordered life. Everything in its place had been his life's motto. The buttons were still there, half the set he needed. It seemed the joy had been in the creating rather than in using them.

It was getting dark and I closed up my bag considering my mission now completed. I had my items safe and secure before the main clearance of the house took place.

To me it was all I wanted.

I locked the door and put the key back into my pocket.

Taking a pained look back at the house, I took in my last breath of the thick air and savoured my last scented memories before setting off for home, a three-hour drive.

When I arrived back I took out my items, now out of place in such a modern setting. I was aware of the change in the background sounds from wind in the trees to cars and chatting. This had always been the difficult transition; I call it my 'rural and urban' trauma.

The items lay for several weeks on the table before I decided what I had to do with them, before I could again cope with the memories they brought back.

On a cold November evening, I eventually took my hoard from where it had been abandoned and put it carefully on the passenger seat in the car.

The journey was uneventful yet I was both apprehensive and cautious; aware that I was carrying my past beside me, now out of context.

He was sitting there quietly and settled in his room. He barely acknowledged me as I sat beside him and took his hand. I placed each of the items on his small table and within view of his now turning gaze. For a brief moment, ever so brief, his eyes showed recognition and warmth. He was with me back on the croft, smiling and touching the buttons, the driftwood and cap badge, exchanging only a few words.

He was once again my grandfather.

An instance of touch and connection, however short, had been made. He squeezed my hand and held the driftwood tightly.

Mid-sentence, and with a seamless movement, he pulled away, sliding into a world none of us could touch, and again became victim to the terrible illness that had taken him from me.

THE DATE

Maria Croce

We clicked – then we clacked. Sharing everything and also nothing.

A flick on a screen. You felt so right – when you should have been left. It would have been virtually impossible to meet on a street. So it was a match made in the cybermarket of love.

We played text tennis for days – set on building up to a meet. Swapping selfies and memes while I picked out a rosy future that included tables for two and weekends away.

Flanter experts, innuendo king and queen, we spoke for hours, and I revealed too much, thinking my expectations were under wraps. You were an expert in undercover work – detecting what I wanted to hear while peeling off the layers of protection around my hungry heart.

When we finally met in person, dilated pupils, an electric touch and a bellyful of butterflies caused a dilution of my resolution to behave. We hit a bar and giggled like teenagers in a booth as we drank cocktails and snacked on olives while you lent in to kiss me. We laughed as we shared dating stories, and you ran your fingers up my back.

That time I nearly killed a first date five minutes after meeting – when I accidentally ran a red light with him as a passenger in the front and a car clipped my wing. I certainly made an impact on him. He survived unscathed – but our romance was pronounced dead at the scene.

Then the long-distance date you met half-way and didn't want to see again. But she discovered her motor was locked in a car park overnight. After a couple of hours trying and failing to find someone to help release her car, she asked you to take her home with you and then drive her the 90 minutes back to her car the next morning. You checked her into a hotel and checked out of the romance.

We bonded as we discussed the ones who had lied about their age, their marital status and their photos.

When the bill came, I offered to split it and you let me. The evening was gone in a flash, and you gripped my hand as we stumbled out into the cold night towards the train station.

Fizz-fuelled and happy I said a prolonged goodbye as we kissed in a shop doorway. We arranged to meet again in a week, and I stepped out into the night to catch my train not realising I was returning to the real world.

No longer strangers thanks to the spark of attraction and the familiarity born from a fortnight of intense messages and calls. I felt it had gone so well.

I messaged to say I'd had a great time. You didn't.

I texted to ask if you were okay. You didn't.

There had been fire – but you left me in a smoke of confusion, with my pain and embarrassment. No explanation. Someone I no longer knew. Someone I'd never known. I wondered if something had happened to you. However, you were alive on social media. But our potential was dead.

You were now a ghost.

THE BASEMENT

Gillian Bowman

Bad attitude

The concrete ceiling was green with moss; the red door that led back into the house locked. Chloe stood in an almost empty room with only the bare essentials needed to survive – water, canned provisions, a toilet and basin in the corner. Dark and dingy, a breeze came from somewhere, gently blowing the light, so it swayed, casting shadows across the room.

She held her knees and arms, sore from where she had hit the floor. Looking up at the ceiling she tried to imagine she had X-ray eyes, and could see several floors above, to the place she had felt welcomed not long ago.

She thought of him, holding her hand as he led her down the stairs to this place. She hadn't trusted him, but she couldn't let go.

And yet, here she was. Alone.

She felt the back of her neck bristle and looked into the shadowy corners. A small red light blinked back at her. There was a camera taped to the ceiling in the far corner of the room.

Her hair tickled her face; she felt a breeze.

Putting her hand on her chest, she turned her gaze to the camera, unmoving, the light blinking. She went to the red door. She banged on it, but her arms were weak.

She heard his words.

You have a bad attitude. You don't smile, you don't laugh at my jokes. You're too quiet, too moody, too glum.

Don't you think there's a problem with your behaviour?

Chloe thought about all the things she did wrong, and all the ways she was wrong. All the ways in which she wasn't loved by anyone. Nobody knew she was down here, and nobody would ask.

She found a worn, thin futon in the corner. She lay down, too anxious to sleep, too weak to move.

Up above, life went on.

Metamorphosis

Weeks had passed. No sunlight. The walls were warping around her.

Sometimes she hallucinated. She saw him in the corner, watching her, taking her hand, comforting her, caring about her. Only to realise there was nothing and break down in despair.

She was sick to the point she was unable to withstand the pain; her body felt like it had been compressed, a grain of sand being crushed by the ocean. For the first time she saw herself from the outside, a small body crumpled on the floor.

The pain of that awareness was like glass cracking under the weight of water.

She felt the concrete under her, the cold on her cheeks, the blood in her veins. She could remember: dancing on the stage, hot water on her skin, steam on her cheeks, the cold night, her cat purring in her lap, an orchard filled with lights, cooking aubergines on the fire, picking walnuts from the trees.

A drop of water hit her cheek. She looked up. The ceiling was leaking. Icy, fresh, coming through the cracks.

Up above, life went on.

In the basement she slowly made peace with silence, with darkness and isolation. She was shedding her former self, the mosaic of moods, tones and interests which mirrored other people's. She imagined her chameleon-like skin lay like a hologram sheet ripped and glitching on the floor.

Her true self was here, in the darkness.

In the time Chloe spent underground, she knew things on the surface were getting duller. She had tried to picture herself up there, but she couldn't remember what up there looked like.

She closed her eyes and thought of him.

I'm sorry.

She could only make him out very far away.

I'm sorry I wasn't better, wasn't healthier, wasn't prettier, or more popular. I'm sorry I didn't act in the right way, at the right times.

I'm getting out, she thought.

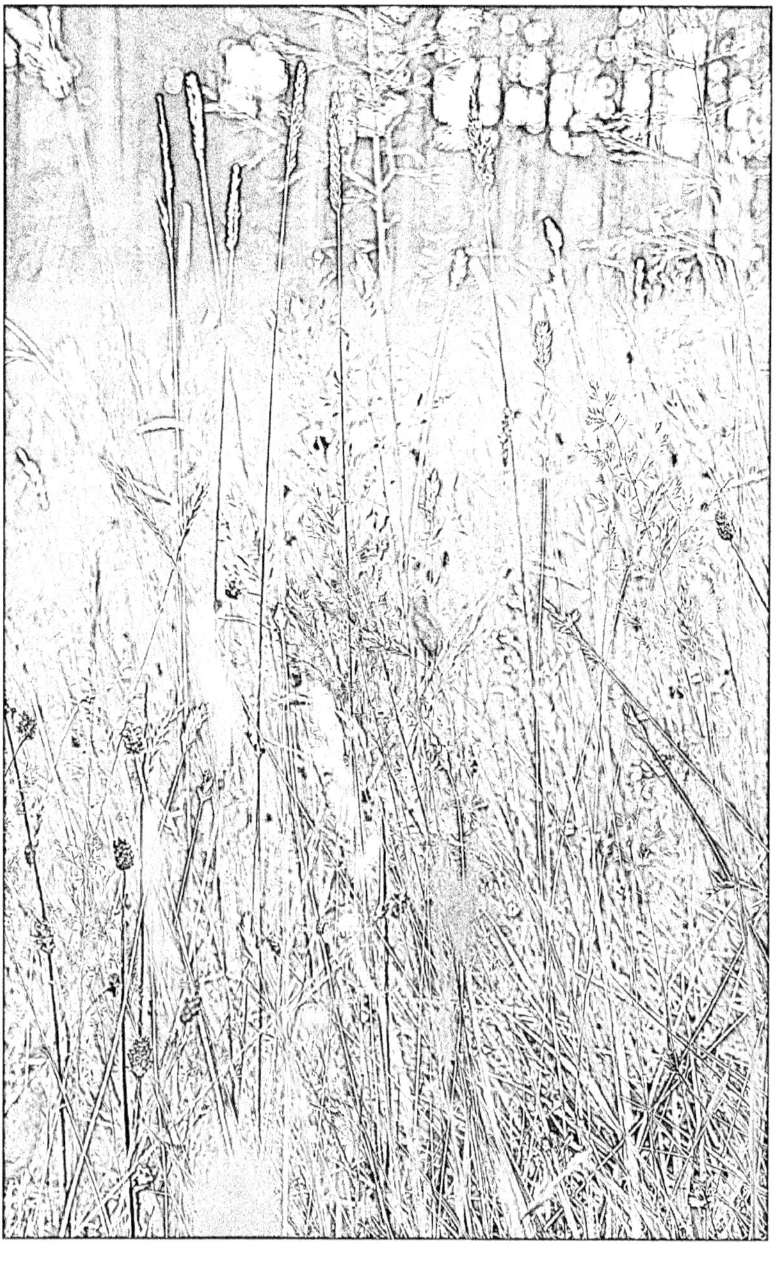

She stood up with purpose, looking for the way out, considering that there might be a way out. She heard a dull mechanical creak. For the first time, the camera in the corner moved.

A voice echoed from a small speaker underneath. It spoke, distorted. His voice?

There's nothing out there for you, remember? Nobody wants you. You can't survive. But I've got you here.

Oh yes, that's right: she wasn't loved by anyone. She remembered.

She sat down – there was nothing out there; she remembered why she sought shelter with him in the first place.

She had been dying, out there. She was mocked and shamed, out there. She didn't want to go outside. She sat back down and closed her eyes.

Soul

Chloe developed an ability to step outside herself, even in the darkest moments. A little cage in her heart opened and she could step out of the darkness, like stepping for a moment outside of the universe, outside the black mass that holds the stars, planets, and galaxies. She couldn't describe the other side – a realisation that nothing matters, and yet everything does. Connected like strings tied between the stars. The argument she had with the man before he took her down here didn't matter, but the feeling that she was in the wrong place, did.

Her life, the one she knew, began to find her again in the shadows. Not the memories that hurt her, but the people who reached out to her, and loved her. They had been hidden in her mind for some time.

She was on the steps outside her gran's home, the breeze in her hair. Chloe had forgotten that there were people out there who cared.

She sat on the bench facing the ocean.

She knew her past. She knew others who used to live in basements, and those who used to make them. Some people did both.

Chloe opened her eyes and took in the dim lighting, the mossy roof, the red door.

She pulled up the chair to reach the camera on the roof and pried it off. She walked to the opposite side of the room where an old wooden hatch stood, the breeze blowing through it. She always knew this was there, but she hadn't thought that perhaps, it would be this easy to walk out.

The lock on the door was rusty – easy to knock open.

Outside, she walked up stairs, and found herself in the cobbled streets of the city.

She didn't want another lecture. She didn't want anyone to tell her how she should think, or how she should feel. She didn't want any more ultimatums. Be this person and we'll accept you.

She was going to move towards the words which were kinder, the eyes which were compassionate, the hands which were tender.

In her hands was the camera from the basement, the light flickering in her hands. She switched the 'off' button, wrapped it in a plastic bag, and threw it in the nearest bin.

INVISIBLE

Lucy Adams

Imagine me a bright starfish or a sea anemone, soft tendrils blowing in the bitter current. Imagine me hard and spiky, soft and exotic. Imagine me a creature from far below the blue watery depths of the sea and you might be able to understand me. But if you ever happened to see me, to really look at the outside of me, you'd never be able to understand what was inside. I've created so many layers, you see. Like laying down sediment. A build-up of millennia of crustaceans deposited on the sea floor. Year after year after year. Until no one remembers the shells and sea creatures that made the grains of sand. And within all that yellowing beauty, there is me, plain and sharp and startling.

Whether I am male or female starts to become an issue early on – it always does. But really I could have been either, a gentle nudge towards X or Y in my father's genetic make-up. That's all it took. And I could have been black or white, tall or short or disabled, or born into abject poverty and abuse, but I was not. I was born white. But for now, imagine me red or purple or orange. Someone with no devastating or defining markings. I am just small and brittle and alone in a sea of colour as infinite as your dreams, and as wide as the world can be seen through one pair of eyes.

I came here to find some kind of answer. Or did I come here to hide? I know it's easy to close my eyes and hold my nose and drift through nothingness, just pedalling my feet and drifting with the current for days. I know because I've done it. There are times and places that if you swim too hard against the tides, you will exhaust yourself and drown. They say if you hit a rip tide the most important thing is not too fight it. There are far more rip tides in far more places than I had realised. And it is hard to see, to really see, when the light is misdirected into wavy lines as soon as it hits the surface of the water.

As a child, I thought I could win dominion with sweet-toothed charm and the imagination of fairies. That only works while you swim within the confines of your own pool, though. Believe me. I've tried. But there comes a time too, after watching pearly white shells settle and crumble into sand, and big fish eat small fish until they are gobbled by sharks for what seems like millennia, that the drifting becomes too much and there is a choice between lying down on that sandy floor or stepping out of the water and looking for another perspective. So that is how I blew in to Gold Coast, like gnarled driftwood. And everywhere I looked, I saw new things and black faces. And it was here that I met her first.

Sometimes, though, you have only to meet a person once for them to become an indelible mark. A permanent bruise. She eroded part of me, cut through the spines to find flesh, but then she scored me and branded me; her actions as searing as the white-hot iron they used to brand the slaves. And after I had been destroyed by her, and by the knowledge of what man will do to man for money, I slipped away back to the sea on the agreement that I would tell no one of what I had seen. But that comes later, much later.

Before that, I had thought I would be able to escape by travelling to one of the colonies. I'd thought the searing sun, leafy banana trees and tropical height would have heightened my appreciation of life. But no one is able to escape themselves. So that is why I am writing it down for you. We will never meet. How could we? And you will already know more than I can ever tell you but I needed to write it down for myself too, to try to be honest. Just look at the outside and you will never see what is inside. Who could know from looking at a man what he is capable of? How deeply he can feel. And that is a man. Imagine trying to guess the core of a woman. Whatever you think you see, you can't see me.

THE DARKNESS

Keith Davidson

She was coping with pretty much everything except the darkness.

The darkness was hard.

One of the consequences of the accident that had killed the engine tech nearly two months previously, was a failure in a minor, non-critical subsystem: the lighting. There was an easy fix but access to the relevant wiring was outside the ship, shielded behind its ceramic outer layer and metal panels underneath.

Now she was alone, going EVA was strictly prohibited. All through training, this has been drummed into her class by tutors. They made it very clear that of course there were space cowboys who would tell you how they did it, that the risk was overstated and that it wasn't a problem.

"But the ones who didn't make it back inside the vehicle are now frozen bags of biomass, slowly spinning around in the void," said the tutors who quickly moved on to survivorship bias.

She listened to the tutors.

Why the lighting couldn't be remedied from inside the ship was something she thought about a great deal. Her conclusion was that with a collection of complex systems like a space vehicle, everything that could go wrong would eventually go wrong and in the wrong order. So no matter how many redundancies and safety features were built in, there would be problems. You just had to hope they didn't go wrong at precisely the wrong time and kill you, like they killed the engine tech.

That said, the ship remained largely functional, despite the accident. It was still on course, the engines appeared fine, the life support was supportive, comms were available and the replicators continued to replicate. Air and water were nominal. She loved being able to use that word in context. Nominal. She never knew what it meant when she was a kid.

When she asked the replicator for dozens of LED torches so she could properly illuminate the flight deck, the replicator had simply flashed up a message about scarcity of resources and popped out a single LED torch.

She even asked for candles at one point, reasoning it was an acceptable risk when she took into account the darkness and her mental health. In response, the interface displayed a laughing-until-crying emoji and the letters GTF.

The candles were a long shot. This was a spaceship after all and naked flames were contraindicated. She didn't understand GTF though. A little more digging revealed that the systems interface for the replicator had been designed in a place in Scotland called Dundee. Once she got back on Terra, she resolved to fly to Dundee, find the interface designer and, in accordance with guidance from a Scottish dictionary, 'Smack him in the coupon.'

It wasn't pitch black: there were stars outside, blinking lights on the controls, the blue glow from each of the flatscreens and a riot of colour when she watched some tube. She was confident she would make it back to Terra without a breakdown – only around two-and-a-half months more to endure.

She definitely wouldn't have managed in the darkness had the engine tech still been aboard.

In the days after the accident she wondered what to do and looked to the manuals for guidance. There were no good choices. In a larger ship, it was recommended that the body be secured in an airlock with the temperature allowed to fall to minus twenty, so it was still in relatively decent shape when it got home. In a small ship with one airlock, and one surviving person aboard, this procedure was similarly recommended.

In situ, that would mean living with the engine tech's corpse within a few metres, albeit on the other side of a door, for more than four months. She couldn't.

On the one hand were the feelings of his family and friends to take into account – also the inevitable questions that would arise at the inquiry.

"Why did you dispose of the body? What do you have to hide?"

On the other hand there was the reality of living in close proximity to a dead man. The engine tech went EVA from the airlock 66 million kilometres ago.

When she bagged his personal effects a day or two later, she felt like a bitch. But looking at them from one waking cycle to the next was hardly doing her any favours and her primary responsibility was to get herself and the ship back to Terra.

She stowed his stuff in a locker by his bunk. They weren't really allowed to take much onboard so space wasn't a problem.

When that thought occurred to her, "Space wasn't a problem," she laughed for the first time since the accident.

HOME AGAIN

Sam Phipps

“I can’t believe it – you never rang once,” Brian said. “Not once the whole day even though you knew that’s all I asked. A word, a kind word, a question to see how I was when you knew I was feeling so bad I could hardly stand it.”

“But I didn’t know you wanted to speak to me,” Vanessa said. “I had to get out myself – it was arranged, remember? We agreed it was OK for me to go and see Caitlin. She’s an old and dear friend and she needed me and we arranged it last week and you said this morning – just go, I'll be fine. Just go, you said."

Vanessa regretted using 'old and dear friend' as soon as it left her mouth. The words sounded bad enough but the inversion made them false and old-fashioned and she knew Brian would take it one way: that she valued Caitlin over him.

"Yes but I thought you knew what a state I was in. Going is one thing but not ringing all day – all day! – fucking hell Vanessa! Is that what you think of me? That I'm worth so little it's OK to see your stupid friend when I'm suffering on my own all day and you don't even ring?"

"I told you," Vanessa said. She felt more than nervous now; it was nausea and she started shifting her weight from foot to foot like some stricken bird. She knew how this would play out – not the exact details perhaps but the route, the package. Nothing she did or said from this point, nothing, would stop what was coming.

"I'm sorry if you're hurt..."

"If? If? There's no if about it Vanessa!"

"Well I'm sorry you are hurt."

"Too bloody right Vanessa. I'm so upset it makes me question why we're together. What's the fucking point if you can't give me – if we can't give each other – what we need."

"But you said..."

"*But you said, but you said...*"

Brian had put on his sarcastic voice, the one that always knotted Vanessa's stomach that bit more. He was shouting now too, coming closer to Vanessa and she hunched her shoulders, stepped back. That voice tapped into a reservoir of all the other times down the years when he'd spoken in that exact same way. Its force was multiplied. It could not pass as an isolated moment to be handled; it had cumulative heft.

"I'm sorry! I'm really sorry I upset you. It's just that..."

"It's just that what?"

"It's just that..." But she couldn't find the words, any words, and Brian stared into her wet eyes and pale face.

"Er, excuse me, why are you crying? I'm the one that should be crying here, not you. I can't believe it! First you do what you've done – or *not* done more like: not phoned me, not come back with a kiss or a hug or a friendly smile – then you fail to explain that in any way at all..."

"But I said..."

"Oh for fuck's sake, Vanessa, you said nothing! That's the whole point – you said nothing."

Vanessa was crying now, trying to swallow sobs, spluttering.

"Look at you Vanessa. You're pathetic. No idea how to make a man happy, how to make me happy. Only interested in yourself. I can't believe you're doing this to me. It's literally fucking unbelievable."

"Oh Brian, please don't do this. Please!"

She put a hand to his shoulder and withdrew it at once, fearful of what it would provoke. He brushed the spot on his brown jumper with his fingertips, a flick you might use to remove dust or dandruff, maybe an ant.

"You know what, Vanessa?"

"What? What?"

"You make me sick. I can't stand looking at you. I still can't believe what you've done – turned it round so we're all meant to feel sorry for you. Instead of looking at how you've hurt me. What are you going to do now? Ring your dear old friend and tell her how mean I've been? It's actually pathetic. You know that, don't you? It's embarrassing."

* * *

Vanessa wandered and wandered because she did not know where to go and everywhere had become the same. Brian's face. Brian's voice. Her replies, non-replies. His shouts. "Oh why don't you just get out if it's so hard being with me!"

She walked round the park, then came to the gate and went round again, head down in the light rain. She thought about contacting her friends, her sister. Caitlin? No chance, she'd been telling her to leave Brian for more than a year. Debbie? Her sister had problems of her own, young kids to put to bed. What about turning up outside Aisha's? Too much for her – it would be too much for Aisha to see her like this. Vanessa always felt Aisha sort of looked up to her, she didn't know why. With Aisha she was like a sensible older sister – the pattern had formed early on and that's the way it was.

She reached an open part of the park, glanced up. This wasn't happening, was it? She was afraid of going home, couldn't see how she could ever negotiate it. Brian's eyes on her the moment she was through the door. She couldn't stand more vitriol, drama. Yet nowhere to go. And how long had she been in this city? Twenty, was it 25 years? No parents. Friends who at the sight of her like this would freak out, wouldn't they? Not believe her, maybe. Laugh at her even. That expanse of grass in the dusk, with the tenement lights ahead, the homes of strangers, made her cry out loud. She thought of ideal families and checked herself – stop comparing, stop comparing. She thought of miserable families and that didn't help either.

The gate again. She couldn't go round a third time. Why not? It made no difference. Nothing made any difference. She may as well try something else to see if she was right. She left the park and headed north. God, she was hungry. What to eat? A carry out? Stuffing herself on the pavement in the winter dusk? Then it hit her. She didn't want food, she didn't want drink, she didn't want Brian. She wanted to disappear. Stop it, stop it. Get some food. You're hungry, it's affecting your brain. No one is going to think straight if they haven't eaten that long and they're dealing with something like this. For fuck's sake Vanessa, get some food – Brian's voice again. For fuck's sake, get out. *For fuck's sake, for fuck's sake, for fuck's sake.*

Her eyes kept being drawn down a yard or two in front of her feet. She was aware of shuttered shops, a few fast food places with fluorescent lights so aggressive she sped up to pass the glare. She almost walked into an old man with a black mini dachshund – had to sidestep two paces to avoid the lead. She expected him to scowl or even swear at her but he gave a kind smile and they passed. Look where you're going, Vanessa, for fuck's sake, look where you're going. She saw the pavement ahead was empty, only a few cars passing. She cried openly now, she cried aloud. She did not know where to go. She wanted to disappear. She didn't want to disappear. She wanted to disappear.

* * *

All the while she was walking, walking. The rain had steadied – at least no one would see her tears. Huh, there was no one around and even if there had been, who would have cared?

She kept seeing herself as she knew he saw her – as he told her he saw her. His conviction was so extreme, his judgement so harsh. She felt squeezed, invalidated. It was more than defensive, it was precarious, a sense of being pressed, strung out, slapped. How could whatever she had done or not done warrant this? It couldn't, she knew that. She knew it rationally but there was something about Brian's ferocity, his swagger, that won out. It filled the space in the flat, in her head, even here in the street. Her voice did not count, her defence did not count. Yet what was there to defend? Slapped, that was it. Her face felt slapped, shamed, as if his accusations were public. Perhaps they were – there was a good chance some of the neighbours would have heard. And was she meant to feel grateful that with Brian the anger would never turn physical?

No, nobody would care. For an instant as her feet splashed in the puddles, an image from childhood flashed through: walking behind her mother, stamping her little red wellies in the puddles and crying. Her mother turned round and said: "Hurry up and stop whining will you, Vanessa! Nobody cares about you when you're whining like that!"

Whining. See me now Mum! I'll give you whining, you silly old bitch! Despite herself she felt a flicker of a smile. The words had taken her by surprise. This was not whining, she knew that; this was pain as real as she had ever felt. Brian had hurt her, given her no space to make amends for whatever it was, no chance for them both to get through this without more insults, more hurt.

Splash-splash-splash-splash. Her mother's face again: *I'll give you whining, you silly old bitch!* It was even better the second time. Her mother had been dead six years, for goodness sake. Where did that come from? It's not like they'd even got on too badly. Oh, Mum.

Vanessa's breathing was becoming a touch deeper. Her coat was soaked on the outside but the rain had not seeped through. She was warm, her pace more even. Her gaze was higher, she was taking in more of her surroundings. She watched the play of rain under the streetlights, heard it drumming on the parked cars. Ping-ping-ping-ping splash-splash. Blah blah blah blah – Brian's words seemed suddenly weaker, a touch ridiculous. She could see it suddenly: those words were nothing to do with her – they came from him and only he was responsible for them. She did not have to pander to him anymore, she would not pander to him anymore. Maybe she was done with him.

She stopped and looked up at the blue neon lettering: *Luigi's*. There was a throwback. She walked in, the smell magnificent, unchanged across the years.

"One fish supper please."

The woman smiled. "Aye, darlin."

OBSESOPHOBIA

Gemma Cameron

Present day

The aisles were warm and muggy today, not unusual for here, I guess. Bulging shelves, delectables everywhere, the smoky smell of the freshly cooked ham, din of the cutting machines and the familiar noise of the child screaming because mummy or daddy has said, "No!"

And there stood the Christmas tree in all its glory, lights draped, sparkling baubles and candy canes around it. Mesmerised by its beauty, shoppers rubbernecked as they passed, the clashing of their trolleys bringing them back to the present. I hear a disrespectful complaint from a shopper, moaning at the salesperson for not having any more candy canes, clementines, blah, blah, blah, blah.

I want the words, "Isn't this meant to be a time of joy?" to jump off my tongue at them. Not surprisingly, they don't.

The shrill beeping from the tills amalgamates with the chirpy Christmas songs playing through the speakers, the chatting, crying, moaning, laughing of shoppers and the crashing of the trolleys swirling around me. It's as though I'm in a parallel world at this time of year. Don't get me wrong—I love Christmas. Nevertheless, it's inflexible, isn't it?

The guilt of not being with this person or that one, the pressure of who you go to, the feeling of dread, sadness, excitement – all for one day which, quite frankly, usually ends with someone upset because of some family drama. Oh, how I wish to be a child again!

Christmas Eve 1975

School was so exciting at this time of year, all the crafts we got to do, the nativity practices and performances, the choir's days out to the nursing homes, singing, and how happy everyone was – even the grumpiest and strictest of teachers softened at this time of year.

My favourite thing was going to the carnival and getting my bag of 2ps and 1ps to throw onto the floats. It was amazing. I loved it! Always! That cold night – it was only 6pm but to me it always felt late – I'd have my red striped, fluffy woolly hat on, the one my gran had knitted me, and a pair of gloves, sometimes mismatched, to keep the winter at bay. The smell of the fish and chip shop always made me feel hungry even though we'd had our dinner at 5pm. The balloon seller stood with what looked like hundreds of strings protruding from him. I remember wondering, "Why doesn't he float away?"

I longed for one of those magical helium balloons, the big ones! But I understood that no meant no. I knew that £5 was too expensive for our family to afford. Anyway, I'd have probably let go of it by accident or had another older kid nick it from me. They were scary the big kids with their bomber jackets and fags in hand, shouting at each other and swearing as gaggles of them walked past.

The sounds of a million feet pounding the pavement, some slow, some fast and some dragging. The blue lights spinning around, illuminating the trees and darkest spots as we walked to our usual viewing place. They were good at closing the roads but there was always one car that got in trouble for being on the road. It was funny. The occasional siren, piercing the night air, added to the excitement. I'd wave at my friends and my parents would talk to their friends about events past. Then we'd hear the magical sound of the band coming!

"They're coming, they're coming, mummy," I'd scream with excitement.

Mum would hand out our bags of coins – we knew to not throw them all at once, because once they were gone that was it! The band would pass with its booming drums, tooting trumpets and showmanship of the leader, spinning and twirling their stick as they walked past. It had started!

Next the teenagers on skates would come with collection buckets dressed in various funny costumes. We loved putting money in their buckets! Then the procession of floats would come. Some had bands playing on them, others had dancing and some I just didn't understand! The smell of the floats in the air was thick and stinky, exhaust fumes from the engines being pushed too far by the weight bearing down on them. There was the sound of the cheering and whooping, singing, laughing and shouting of names as children ran into the road to pick up coins that had missed the floats – or sweets not yet claimed, chucked from the floats by other gleeful children.

My sister took part one year. I can't quite remember what she was but I think it was with the Guides. I was part of the Brownies and we didn't have a float. I'd have loved to have done it. I think she had great fun. I remember my mum being pretty stressed on the day as she had to get to the start at a certain time – a lot earlier than we normally went – as the floats were marked and lined up. I remember being a bit afraid as it was so busy and there were lots of people. My mum tightened her grip on my hand saying, "Don't let go."

That year there was a lot – and I mean a lot – of walking! It slips my mind as to whether my sister won anything for her float but it wouldn't have mattered anyway. Luckily, it was on a Friday as we always got home very late and had to quickly brush our teeth and jump into our pyjamas and get to bed. Sometimes we'd still get a story – if we got into bed quick enough.

With the carnival done it meant it was getting so near to Christmas! I loved Christmas, as every child did. I remember writing my list to Santa and posting it on the way to school! Where did those letters actually go? School would end and there'd be a week until Christmas Day! We'd go to garden centres to visit Santa and go shopping for last minute or forgotten gifts. The crowded shops didn't bother me back then, not like they do now, that's for sure. Then before you knew it, Christmas had come and gone and you were having to go back to school to start a new year. It was over in a blink of an eye. Just like it is now but with no stress, responsibility or guilt! Grandparents, now all passed, were there too, I miss that.

Present day

I love looking at the beautiful, cute and glistening Christmas decorations in the non-food aisles. In fact, I really like the non-food aisles the best. The toys, new books which I've not seen before, and the magazines – often choosing a gardening mag to take home. Yes, these aisles I don't mind. But alas, this is not what I'm here for. Once a month, maximum, I visit the supermarket.

Old habits linger in the dark, emotions fighting with each other like dogs fighting over a bone. The list I've written, left on the fridge, is no use now. I go up and down the long, daunting aisles with a ball and chain on my legs, causing my feet to scrape into the floor, the cold patterned concrete gathering up under them. The audacious, spine chilling, hideous ghouls protruding from the shelves daring me to take from them. Their beady hollows, directed at me, stand out. The gnawing in my gut, flight mode activated. Slowly I drag myself around, trying not to look at these abominations, totally aware that they in fact are not real and no one else is experiencing this.

Confliction: my delightful, alluring, courageous angel pulls me up out of the concrete, releasing the cold, damp, piercing chains and blowing away the supercilious ghouls long enough for me to look and grab what I need. But still the gnawing, gut-wrenching sensation remains – how I wish it didn't. It's been 20 years now, and yet, here I stand still in this headspace. This is what people don't get. These things remain for life, not through my lack of effort, or not being well, but just because my brain remembers and likes to guilt me every chance it can. My internal battle is daily – but here it's at its worst.

Sometime in 1978

At nine years old, a skinny, athletic, sporty, non-academic me dislikes school but loves PE. Goal-driven, being pushed by dad to play my best, losing meant being emotionally bashed by him, telling me how rubbish I am, while mum of course never said these things, reminding him that it's only a game. The cruel mocking at dinner – from all, for losing – splinters and echoes in my head.

"You're a loser"; "You may as well die"; "It's a boys' sport anyway"; and "You're an idiot," twirl around and around me. I'm dizzy with emotions, sad and angry and hurt that this was my family and I'd let everyone down, even though there is no I in team. Even to this day the hurt remains and I wish I'd had a more supportive atmosphere to grow up in, instead of being pounded, broken and fractured into tiny insignificant pieces – pieces I have to try to pick up again and piece back together.

Antithetically, if we won, it was all praise and happiness from him. Even now I strive for perfection, after having it drummed into me that nothing else is good enough in this world, which, of course, I now know is wrong. In spite of that, it still haunts me. One conversation, which was had repeatedly, loiters in my head.

"That girl is so fat," remarks my brother. Sniggers from my dad and sister, heard as they eat their dinner.

"Why would you even want to live being that fat?" remarks my dad, while my brother blurts out, "She is so fat, she must eat like ten dinners a day!"

"Stop it!" shouts my mum, "that's really mean!"

"You been to your keep fat class today?" my dad says, vindictively.

Hurt, I see my mum's head drop, emotionally hit again, in front of us all. I remember feeling really sorry for her.

"Don't be so mean dad," I'd yell.

"Shut up Jemima Puddlefuck," he'd say, laughing as he did, brother laughing too.

My sister kept her head down knowing she would be targeted soon.

But you see, all this fat shaming led me to believe that, in fact, to gain weight was bad – which at nine years old was regrettable. Of course I would gain weight – I was still growing! I exercised as much as I could.

This worked for a while but as the fat shaming continued – and my mum put on weight due to a medication she needed – the emotional abuse grew more vicious and the emotions I felt inside and voices I heard grew stronger, forming my mindset. It fuelled my journey into a lonely, scary and bleak world where I grew perfidious in my ways, lost and alone, clawing out a hollow existence. I couldn't come back from it, losing the few friends I had. Well, I say friends but really they weren't, or they'd have stayed and helped me.

The only release I got was exercise and sport. This grew into an obsession that left me a shadow of my former self. Muscle was being burned and I grew weak, my performance declining, so the emotional bashings grew. By this point, my mum would disappear out of the house. I'd always worry and be upset but this is what I grew up with and this was my reality: men were mean to women and if you were fat you needn't be alive, which terrified me.

Even to this very day when I put weight on, I feel ashamed, and even though I know it's okay, I can't break free. It is my belief that people can be whatever size they like as long as they are happy.

After all, that's what matters, isn't it?

REFLECTION

Lucy Adams

She stands staring at the kitchen window. An old oak tree looks back at her. The oak tree waves his long twisted arms. But she doesn't see. She looks down instead. She has noticed a piece of sweetcorn stuck in the plug hole. She searches for a knife with the right shaped end to take the sweetcorn out. She can't quite get the correct angle. Her elbow is constricted. A stack of dirty dishes gets in the way. Damn, she says. Damn, damn, damn.

A shadow dances outside the pane of glass. It is a leaf child shadow with small pointed ears. Ears of ash. Not leaves. Just their shadows. She pulls a fork from the dirty pile. The top plate topples. Is about to fall. Then rights itself. Without her doing anything. She wonders at how it didn't fall. She is accustomed to thinking she is the only one who makes things happen. But she doesn't take her time to think about it.

She digs the fork into the tiny hole but succeeds in only spearing the sweetcorn and getting the prong stuck. It bends. She doesn't notice she is holding her breath. The leaf child dances faster. Reaches towards the glass. She sees red onion, bits of pinkish chicken skin, greying fish scales, browning broccoli, old petals stuck too. She wonders at how the colour of food changes with decay. And how long it has sat there unnoticed. All stuck in the plug she should have cleaned out months ago.

She tugs at the fork, sees the prong bend. Pulls. She leans in to get more leverage and widens her stance. Cranes her neck to look closer at the details of the plug. The leaf child dances faster. And faster. She reaches towards the dark house. Moving closer. Arms of sycamore, rowan and elm. Eyes of beech nuts. Hair of willow. The woman swears beneath her breath. The oak shakes his head in dismay. The fork comes loose and she falls backwards onto the cold tiles just as the child reaches the door. And turns to shadow. Again.

She lies on the floor. Looking at the ceiling. Thinking about the spots that need re-painted. All the jobs she hasn't done. All the moments wasted. Not knowing she missed the whole show. Outside in the grove of oak and elm, the witch sighs. The child and the old witch dissolve back into the woods.

WELFARE CALL

Anthony S. Holroyd

You would scarcely have known it was there. Perched above placid burn; dwarfed by conifers; steep mountain slopes flanking either side.

The glen was enough of a surprise, a gap – a quick glance at green pasture between the mountains. Its narrow mouth, a steep gorge with small fields visible above, belied its expanse. A world unto itself – miles and miles of it running for an hour or more, a solitary ribbon of twisting tarmac and loose gravel winding its way endlessly into the very heart of nowhere. All the while passing field and forest and occasional cottage.

This cottage was one such – caught as flashes of brilliant white through the roadside trees: deciduous, wider, more verdant, more revealing – not observed so much as acknowledged, unconsciously. A mental note scrawled messily in the margins of the mind.

The driveway was a nightmare. Loose rocks and stones over several hundred yards. Steep climbs, sharp turns, and no way of telling whether you were about to be plunged into the burn or head-on into the grill of an opposing vehicle.

Still, she'd driven here plenty enough to know that he couldn't drive anymore, and the chances of a visitor were slim to none.

Indeed, as her trusty hatch carried her over the last hillock she could see, in the corner, his old Land Rover slowly becoming one with the earth. Weeds and creepers clinging to its flanks; its body rusting, hollowing out; the soil beneath stained with oil and a ruddy oxide hue.

She parked where she always did. Over to the left, by the old outbuilding – slowly weathering to rubble. Trees and thickets rising proud out of the tired dykes.

The cottage remained, as yet, unconquered. The walls finished in brilliant white, the roof heavy and steeply canted – diving in severe, slate grey towards the low, heavy set window frames. The squat little door sat squarely centred under the austere roof. Uninviting, but unintimidating.

She pushed open the porch doors. Windowless – wooden. The paint starting to buckle and bubble and peel from a long, damp winter. Beyond, almost all frosted glass, the inner door would lead her to the hallway. She could make out the beige carpet and dark wood walls – back lit as grey daylight streamed lazily through from the kitchen beyond.

She rapped her fingers on the soft, textured glass. It was dull and resonant. A film of dirt and dust and lichen she had dared disturb wrapped around her knuckles. Even here the earth encroached. The cottage was not conquered, perhaps, but it was besieged.

"Hello? Mr. McEwan? Hello?"

Her knuckles rapped again. The dust rose – dull, blunt and stale.

"Hello Wullie? You've no run away on me, have ye?"

No response. No matter. She backed through the porch door and turned to the terracotta plant pot on the right. What it had once nurtured was anyone's guess, but today its drowned, black soils were home to any number of nameless, feral mosses. Behind and beneath was her prize. Coarse and half rusted she pulled it from its stagnant pool. The lock took some persuading that this was, indeed, a key, cut for it and only it, but at last relenting. The door swung lazily, gracefully across the carpeted hall.

"Wullie? It's just me, Leigha, I'm just checking in?" Her voice once again cut through the dank, pregnant silence.

The living room was off the right of the hall. It was dark and cavernous – the blinds being pulled too.

She entered, hugging the walls – she made her way instinctively to the window frame; grabbed two handfuls of dank, heavy fabric and pulled the curtains forcefully, decisively open.

"How've you been managing Wullie? Up to anything new or just the same as usual? Leg no giving you too much bother I hope?"

She turned – he was sitting in his armchair, as always. He sat tall, proud. Whisps of grey hair errant and chaotic. His shirt, un-ironed but worn with quiet dignity. He did not look up to meet her gaze.

She paused, took a deep breath and then smiled sadly, tacitly. "Of course, Mr. McEwan – let me get some air in here for you."

Her fingers wrapped around the rusted metal fittings and with some effort she wrestled the window open in uneven, jerking movements. "There, fresh air – liberating?", she insisted.

"I need to make a quick phone call to some of my colleagues, just to keep them up to speed. May I use your landline?...

... It's in the kitchen, isn't it? ...

... After that's done, I'll get some of this clutter away for you?"

He sat stoically, unmoved.

Leigha made for the kitchen, closing the door behind her. She reached for the old Bakelite telephone on the wall. How did they ever call anyone on these stupid old things? She wondered under her breath. Having spent a few moments reacquainting herself with the rotary dial she lifted the receiver to her ear, leaning back against the old worktop as dull, distant tones rung out in procession.

The call was unremarkable, quick, matter of fact. She spoke softly, earnestly.

"Of course, I'll let you in..."

"Yes, the wee white cottage on the left... aye, you know the one..."

"Could you send someone round for Mrs. Henderson? I'll not have the chance to see her now, today..."

"Yes, I'll keep him company until you get here..."

Leigha replaced the phone and made her way swiftly back to the living room. Immediately she busied herself with the clutter on the low, wooden table in front of him.

"Don't mind me, I'll just get this mess sorted out for you," she insisted cheerfully. She separated plates and mugs from old newspaper articles and crosswords. The crockery she took directly to the drainer, balancing expertly on both arms, "years of practise, Wullie," she explained with a wry grin. "Teenage years waiting tables and..." she chuckled to herself, "teenagers of my own who would be more at home using a trough."

A moment later she had returned to the pile of papers, "I'll just find a space for these, I don't presume there would be a problem with popping them in one of the drawers in the cabinet?"

The cabinet stood behind the door – a relic of dark, polished wood; glass and faded, bluing brass.

She busied herself folding the various miscellany into the two lower drawers. Once finished, she stood (with some assistance from the large, brass handles) and found herself eye to eye with another woman. The woman was dressed smartly, a tight coat tugging at her midriff, pulling it neatly into shape. Her hair, too, was tight – curled to within an inch of its life, and for all that effort hidden coyly behind a well fitted, felt cloche. She smiled, a prim and proper smile – dark, painstakingly painted lips drawing sharp relief from alabaster skin. Behind her sat a man: young, lanky and handsome.

Shirt, blazer, and boater hat all perfectly creased and perfectly correct. His weighty, well-cut jaw had broken into a broad and irrepressible grin.

"She was beautiful, you both were," Leigha said as she turned from the photograph. "Elsie, did you say her name was? I'm sorry I never got the chance to meet her."

Mr. McEwan sat stoically, staring at nothing in particular.

"How many years has it been, if you don't mind me asking?" she asked, tentatively.

"Must've been at least a decade or more," she said, answering herself. She moved to sit on the couch by the window, catching sight of the photographs on the mantelpiece as she did. "And your boys – you must be so proud of them? Where's Alex these days? Abu Dhabi, isn't it? He must be making a fortune out there..."

She trailed off.

"I don't suppose you've had much chance to see him... or John? I can't even remember where you told me he was. I'm sure they love their dad very much but, well, it's not like you've been able to travel. And there aren't exactly direct flights from all four corners of the world to this wee glen in the back of beyond."

She hesitated, perhaps that was a little too blunt? Too insensitive?

Her charge, thankfully, didn't seem to be at all bothered. Perhaps he wasn't as quick with an opinion as she was used to.

"I'm sorry, I didn't mean to be blunt I just... how did you do it?" She didn't mean to stop there, but her mouth was running faster than her thoughts... she let her question settle with the dust.

Muted silence answered.

"Sorry, I'm not good at putting on airs and graces, I never have been – my husband always says I put the 'B' in subtle..."

She hesitated again – why though? He had no objection?

"I mean...you've always been happy, or happy enough. Perhaps happy is the wrong way of putting it?"

She thought for a moment, "Content, comfortable – even now, at peace. How? How have you kept it up? You know I think I might've gone mad if I were you! Years in this cottage all by myself? I'd have gone properly mental in a few months! . . . sorry! I..."

That was maybe a bit tactless, she thought.

"Maybe I'll make myself a cup of tea, if you wouldn't object?"

No objections, nor admonishments, came, so she promptly stood and excused herself back into the kitchen.

A cup of tea would clear her head. It usually did – for a while at least. She reached inside her kit bag for her mug. It was her mug: not much to look at these days – paint faded and bleached through the years – but it was hers. Her daughter, Charlie had made it – well, decorated it (but that's what counts) – many years ago, when she was still at primary school. She held it tight in her left hand, her coarse palm resting on the cool porcelain, and smiled wistfully as she remembered the excitement with which her daughter had bounded up to her all those years ago.

"This is for you mummy, I made it myself!"

"Did you really? All by yourself Charlie?"

"Well… I painted it for you."

"Aww sweetie! I'd say that was the most important job! Oh it's lovely! This is my new favourite…"

She wondered how Charlie was finding college all those miles away. Charlie was still every bit as full of life as always, she told herself, she'll be doing grand… just wish she'd call her old mum a little more often.

Leigha set the mug down on the worktop – the metallic clunk of her ring on the hard ceramic pulling her bodily out of her reverie. Why was she still wearing that thing? she thought, a little disappointed in her own sentimentality. True, she was still married but David hadn't lived at home in months. Still at his sister's? He must be. I wonder if he's winding her up as much as he did me?

The kettle began to whine plaintively on the stove top. That was hot enough. Leigha knew from experience that if she let the kettle boil, she'd have to let the tea cool down – and something would undoubtedly come up in that time to divert her. By the time she returned the tea would be lukewarm at best, or otherwise stone cold. No – let the kettle start to whimper, then drink the tea immediately. She returned to the living room, grasping the mug with both hands and sat again.

"I'm sorry I was so blunt," she said after some thought.

"It's just something I've been thinking about quite a lot lately." She let each sentence hang, thinking carefully about what she said next.

"My daughter, Charlie, she... she's just left to go to uni, well it was last year but, I worry about her. I worry that she's making friends, I worry that she's studying properly, that she's eating, that she's warm, that she's safe..."

Leigha thought back to her last conversation with her daughter. It had been a little after Christmas, not more than a couple of weeks after Charlie had gone back to uni for the start of term. David had been around for Christmas day and Hogmanay, but it had become plainly obvious to Leigha that Charlie was just a little too perceptive for them to keep up any kind of pretence. Kind as she was, Charlie hadn't said too much about it, she'd well-judged that it was something neither of her parents had wanted to talk about over the festive season – and certainly not something that they wanted to discuss in each other's company. Instead, a few quiet words with mum to confirm her suspicions sufficed and she was back off to the other end of the country and her studies. Now, after weeks of radio silence, weeks in that silent, empty house, Leigha had decided she needed to hear her daughter's voice again.

"Oh, hi mum?"

"Hi Charlie."

"It's... Charlotte please mum, I've told you that... is everything okay?"

"Yes, yes all's well! Just wanted to check in on my little girl – see how she's settling in?"

"It's been the best part of a year mum; I settled in a while back."

"Oh... of course, I just wanted to be sure – you're not needing anything, are you? Food? Clothes? A little extra cash?"

"No mum, like I said at Christmas, I'm fine."

"Okay... good, good..."

"How's dad?"

"Your father? He's eh... he's fine."

"Still on Auntie Josie's couch then?"

"Erm... yes – for the time being. I'm sorry Charlie, I just needed... well you know how he can be and I just needed... I needed a little space is all. You know your father can be a bit much sometimes."

"He means well, mum."

"I know, and... I know that Charlie..."

"It's Charlotte, mum."

"Sorry, yes, of course! I know he means well I just... that doesn't stop him from being too much sometimes and he's just... he's just too much right now."

"Okay, well I hope you two figure it out... sooner rather than later for all our sakes."

"I know honey, I hope we figure something out too."

"Look mum... I've got to go, some of the society girls are having prees at the Ballroom and Meghan and I were going to join them."

"Ahh Meghan, that's your flatmate, isn't it?"

"Yeh, she is – anyway, I really have to go now mum. Lots of love."

"Bye then..."

"Yeh, bye – speak later."

And that had been it, maybe three minutes and Charlie was off again. Out with friends.

"She's not a bad kid or anything, Wullie," Leigha said, quickly defending her daughter. "She's kind and thoughtful really – just young and... well I suppose it's all new to her just now. A new city, new people, new places and things to see and do and try. Her life must be so full right now... just wish she'd call her old mum a little more often."

She let the thought hang in the dusty air between them.

"Did Elsie miss your boys when they left? I suppose she must have. Never easy having an empty house...I suppose you must have missed her terribly too, when she went ... and then all alone in this house." She looked around, "Cosy enough, but even this place must've felt lonely," she thought.

"Maybe I need to take a leaf out of your book, eh?" she said, brightening for a moment, "You did a not bad job looking after yourself – keeping yourself right, eh?"

She stopped, snorted and shook her head.

"You know, I've spent my whole life looking after other people. My patients, my kids... God! Even my David would've starved long ago but for my efforts! Don't get me wrong Wullie, I love it. It's who I am to help. I canna tell you how happy it makes me, how proud I've felt even just being a hand to hold or an ear to talk off. I've always loved being there for other people, but I guess it means I've never had to be there for myself. I've just focused on what other people need from me, and I'll get round to sorting myself out when I have time. Usually that involves a microwave dinner, eaten standing over the sink of the breakroom in the 20 minutes I have to myself... or a lukewarm bowl of overcooked stew from the slow-cooker and a quick glass of wine from a three-days-open bottle once the kids were off to bed. I guess with Charlotte off making her way in the world, and David at his sister's I finally have the time. I've perfected looking after everyone else, maybe it's finally time to start learning how to look after myself."

Just then there came a muffled rumble as the door swung open. The man who bustled in was about 50, a little rotund – dressed in two-tone green tweed interrupted with patches of earthen leather.

"Good morning," said Leigha, standing quickly and necking the last dregs of tea. She swiftly returned her mug to her workbag.

"Sorry it took me so long," the new visitor replied, "We had his address on file, but he hasn't been in since I took over the practice... and I've never had a call out, it's an absolute bugger trying to find this place."

"It isn't half," Leigha offered, placatively.

"Right, well I suppose we'd better do this properly," the doctor said, regaining his composure in light of his apologies being accepted.

"Of course. Well, this is Mr. William McEwan, 91. Some difficulties with mobility, lives alone – hence our visits. No degenerative or terminal illness that we know of, he was just a very elderly man – and in pretty good nick for his age as well."

"Well, he certainly had a decent innings," the doctor replied almost jovially.

"I think it must've happened during the night; he was already cold when I arrived," Leigha continued. "I just hope it was quick for his sake, not too painful. I just hope he wasn't frightened, all by himself." She smiled sadly once again. "He wouldn't have been, I don't think. He was a brave soul," she added firmly.

"Any family?"

"Not here – his wife died maybe 10 years ago. He has two sons – one's in Abu Dhabi. The other is somewhere else abroad but I'm afraid I couldn't tell you where. Do you want me to try and get a hold of them?"

"No, no I'll...I'll go through his notes when I get back to the practice, phone them myself. I presume you have quite a few more appointments to get to today anyway? I'll see him the rest of the way."

The doctor, who by this time was busy kneeling and fussing around his patient, looked up as he finished talking and smiled kindly at Leigha.

Leigha smiled back, "I'll phone work and let them know I'm free again – you don't know how right you are! I'll be playing catch-up all shift now but...no rest for the wicked I guess."

"Aye, true enough," the doctor said wryly, as he busied himself once more with his charge.

Leigha – seeing Mr McEwan was in good, kind, and capable hands – excused herself. She walked back out into the bright, cold sunlight and breathed in deeply, letting a torrent of air wash through her. She stood for a moment, taking the time to feel the gravel beneath her feet; the stinging breeze on her hands and cheeks – there was something about her. You couldn't say what exactly. Perhaps she carried herself a little taller; perhaps she looked at the world with renewed intent; perhaps she moved a little more deliberately. Whatever it was, until that moment, until now, you would scarcely have known it was there.

SECOND CHANCES

Kirsty Turnbull

The fog was thick around the river. Joe exhaled deeply, trying to calm his nerves, his breath carried away by the icy wind. He fidgeted with the ear covers of his hat, flattening them against the side of his head. He pulled his puffer coat over, shivering from the cold. The zip had broken a few weeks ago, but it was his favourite. It was also the only half-decent jacket he owned. Joe's hands were going numb and he wished he was wearing his gloves. He rummaged around everywhere this morning but he couldn't find them. He didn't want to miss the bus that only came around every hour and a half, so he decided his pockets would have to do.

The church bell tolled in the distance: 11am, the time they had agreed to meet. *They're probably just running a little late, especially with this weather,* thought Joe. His legs started to shake and he fiddled with the stem of the red tulips he had picked from a nearby flowerbed. It wasn't right to pick flowers from the public gardens, he knew that. But if he remembered correctly, tulips were their favourite and he couldn't help picking a couple. There were plenty there; no one would miss them. What if he had remembered incorrectly, though? What if it was daffodils? It had been almost 40 years since they had last seen each other. There was that one time Joe had made peanut brittle, thinking peanuts were their favourite but they were in fact, allergic. Joe shook his head and tried to focus on something else. Had he shaved enough? Did he remember to comb his hair? At least most of the grey was hidden under his hat. Joe shook his head again, deciding to focus on the intermittent footsteps of the passing figures that were merely shadows in the fog.

Joe jumped when he heard a familiar voice say his name. He stood up sharply, almost stumbling, grasping the tulips. He was quiet for a moment, taking in the face he had not seen for decades. There were a few lines and the once dark blonde hair was now platinum. The sparkling blue eyes were still there though, as was the sharp, stubbled jaw and crooked nose from their boxing days. Joe couldn't help but think that his own face had not aged quite so well.

"Edward. Eddie," Joe's voice stuck in his throat, almost in disbelief.

Eddie smiled widely, embracing Joe in a long, warm hug. Joe exhaled deeply, watching his breath cloud and disappear. He had waited a lifetime for this moment.

"I brought you these," Joe said, when they finally pulled apart.

"Tulips," Eddie said brightly, smiling. "You remembered."

Relief flooded Joe, his shoulders relaxing. He grinned, taking Eddie's hand, a warmth travelling through him as they walked into the foggy afternoon.

THE GHOSTS WE CARRY

Sam Phipps

The postie hands me a small stack of parcels and cards.

Is it Sam's birthday?

Monday!

I'll be sad on Monday.

Why will you be sad?

That's my son's birthday.

Why will you be sad?

Before the question is off my lips a second time I realise the answer will be about loss.

Aye, the 9th of October is my son's birthday. Twelve years ago he committed suicide. He was 23.

I'm so sorry to hear that.

An understatement. The postie has been coming up our stair for a few years. I'm shocked at the news, withheld all that time, but the language has jolted me too. Committed? You commit a crime, or a sin – sins of commission, sins of omission, I haven't forgotten that – but not suicide. Especially your own child. If you had the misfortune to have to describe it, wouldn't you say they took their own life? Or even killed themselves? I almost want to correct him, display my non-judgement, compassion, but in those microseconds I stifle the urge.

Every day the postie struggles to reach the top – all 66 steps, not including the front entrance. Going down is maybe even harder. He's a big man, an awkward mover, and his face betrays the effort. But he smiles and jokes and chats. Maybe that's not all social – pausing outside the door and engaging with residents gives him a wee rest.

My son, you and another legend with birthdays on 9th of October – John Lennon!

He manages another smile. A touch embarrassed at making this trio, I place the pile on the ledge inside the front door.

He used that term to me but does he think of his son as having *committed suicide*? Perhaps he leans on it for the distancing effect, a morsel of emotional protection against the loss that is unbearable yet has to be borne. If you think of your child as taking their life or killing themselves, is that too direct, too much to endure? Or maybe the language does not matter one jot next to the reality.

I share a birthday with this man I never met, who took his life at 23. How many others are wandering the streets with the same burden as that man's father, mother, siblings, friends? My cousin Rufus jumped in front of a train at the age of 18 or 19. His mother, my maternal aunt, never mentioned him to me once in the remaining 36 years of her life. Same with his sister.

Another sister responded positively when I mentioned – by email across the world, and in connection with their mother's death – his sense of mischief and told her I thought about him often.

My brothers and I were his big cousins and we teased him when he came to stay with us wearing a padlock around his neck. He was about 14 and the punk posture was comical because the chain had a blue plastic coating, I recall, not the hardcore look of bare metal as seen on Sid Vicious. For the last years of his mother's life, I thought about bringing his name up, but my aunt and I rarely saw each other and it never felt like the right time. It was intolerable the way he'd been erased from conversation, from history, but I was complicit in that for fear of upsetting her. Maybe if I'd had the courage to recall him to her, at the right time, the opportune moment, it would have warmed her, brought us closer, honoured them both. The moment never came.

* * *

Another cousin of mine, on my dad's side, died in the woods in his 30s. He as good as took his own life too. He'd cut himself off from his family, lived alone in a tent for years. They knew he was alive because he drew money from an account – until that stopped. His remains were found months later. He was at least 10 years older than me, the first man I'd spoken to who had hair down to his shoulders, blond hair with a centre parting. I remember his long bony fingers lifting chess pieces when he played our grandmother at her home in Wiltshire. He laughed a lot and had such a gentle disposition.

His father had sent all four sons to the same boarding school he'd hated himself – it's common, that, apparently – and he hated it too. Got expelled for drug use, amyl nitrate I think, and I don't know much else about his life except that he didn't *fit in*. What does that mean? Fit into what? A suit? A job? A label? I think my mum described him to us as a hippy, but I never knew if that was on the basis of the hair alone. I sensed it might also have covered his refusal to conform. My father and his sister – my aunt, this dead cousin's mother – saw little of each other, a distance that was duplicated by the next generation. Formality and awkwardness characterised those rare visits to their big, gloomy box of a Georgian manor house in the countryside. My dad couldn't stand the place.

When I think of that cousin now, the shorthand is almost all I have – long blond hair in centre parting, pronounced Adam's apple, shy, remains found in the woods. Sometimes I get stuck on that last bit and think, what the hell happened? How could that happen? But for the most part it's been absorbed, assimilated. If I was closer to his three brothers I'd want to ask them about him. But I'm not. We mainly see each other at funerals, the odd wedding. I don't have a clue what ceremony, if any, was performed to mark his death. Whatever it was, we weren't invited or informed, and that includes Dad. I don't say that with bitterness, it's more to show the distance. Or the shame.

* * *

As for that younger cousin, I remember he sent demo tapes to John Peel but didn't get anywhere with them. This was cited at the time as a contributory factor in his death, that and his parents' divorce when he was 10 or 11. As if it's that simple: X plus Y happens therefore you end your life. I wish we'd had the kind of friendship where he picked up the phone and he could have chatted to me or my brother, told us what he was going through. Maybe, just maybe, that might have made the difference. But our meetings, also rare, were still arranged through the mothers and we lived 200 miles apart. Maybe it would not have helped anyway. It's awful to think of his desperation, resignation, the final journey to York station. How did he get there? Did he catch a bus? Did he have a particular train in mind? A bus to take you to *that* train.

The worst thought is that he got his mum to drive him there on some pretext – a record or clothes shop, perhaps.

I wonder about the driver too, whether he ever got over it. We had no idea things had been that bad until it was too late. When my mum told me on the phone, she'd woken me with a student hangover, a landline I had to reach by walking somewhere, and my thumb hurt like hell because I'd caught it in the door the night before. Trifles. I'm pretty sure, but not 100 per cent, that she said *your cousin Rufus has killed himself* rather than the Victorian alternative. I hope so, in a way, though it hardly matters.

It's so difficult to get beyond those kinds of deaths back into the life. I remember him a few years earlier laughing to the point of tears when we kept saying in a silly voice, after rounds of a card game that was new to him: *"And Rufus fails to score..."* That must have been the summer he came to stay with us. He brought his own radio to follow the cricket, Yorkshire or maybe England. He'd hold up the little box to his ear and listen, listen with his big blue eyes.

* * *

The postie is backing off now, preparing for the descent.

To this day I'll never understand why he did it. But my heart aches for him every day, my friend, every day.

With one hand on the banister to counterbalance the heavy satchel, he makes a fist with the other and thumps his heart a few times through the Royal Mail red of his shirt.

OFFICE ORDER

Miriam Landor

Willa went into the admin office and looked across at her old desk. She always had it precisely placed so that she could see both the entrance to the Educational Psychology Service base and the coffee area, with its regulation upholstered seats and constantly-topped-up cake box. Before she passed the timesheets and mileage claims up to Theo, the Principal Educational Psychologist, for signing, she always checked them herself, both for completeness and for veracity. So she needed to see exactly when each member of the team came in, which school files they took out, how long they spent chatting over their break. Of course, it wasn't her place to call out one of the psychologists in a downright lie... But she had her ways of leaving them in no doubt that a wee error, a slip-of-the-pen, must have occurred, which she'd be most happy to put right for them. It amused her to see them crumble, even the older ones.

But to her eyes the desk was now in a chaotic mess, and there was no sign of its current user. Footsteps approached behind her.

"Hey Willa – bet you never thought you'd see me again, eh?"

Willa froze. She knew that voice. A moment later she stiffened further as arms were flung around her.

"Toni! what are you doing here? You're not.... You've not been standing in for me, have you?"

No, she groaned inside, this was her absolute worst nightmare.

"Indeed I have, me ol' mate. Your boss, Theo, called me in when you started your matty leave all in an emergency rush, and luckily I was between jobs, so I started the next day. I was really glad to hear about your twins, by the way – what are they called?"

"Jessica and Jemima – we call them Jess and Jem."

"Super. But what are you doing here? Your matty doesn't end for another month, I was told."

Willa reddened slightly. "I just wanted to check, you know, that everything was ok, that it was all going straight, before I come back. I know I'm not supposed to be here, don't mind me. I won't interfere...."

Toni seemed to doubt whether Willa would be able to prevent herself, her face betraying her feelings. "I'll tell you what, I was just about to stop for a break. Come and sit with me, and we can catch up a wee bit. It's years since I've seen you, not since we left secretarial college, you with your top marks and me, well less said about that the better...." Toni giggled, shaking her purple-streaked curls.

For once in her life, Willa felt badly out of place. This was her office! She had everything organised to a T, and just looking around she could see how things had slipped – empty trays which should have held blank mileage logs, journals lying haphazardly in stacks on half empty library shelves.

Toni was off again.... "And are you still doing that Mensa stuff? We were so impressed when we found that out, our own class genius..."

"Shh," Willa hissed, her eyes wide with alarm. "That was years ago, I never speak about it now." She looked apprehensively around the psychologists' desks, but thankfully they were all out at their schools.

She needed to get her old typing buddy off this topic. "And you Toni, what about you? Still temping?"

"Sure I am. I don't like to get tied down for too long, you know me. But Theo said there will be enough work to catch up with even after you come back, and that he can keep me on another few months. We'll be a team, you and me! What fun, hey?"

Willa blenched. Was Theo losing his marbles? Pretty, bubbly Toni could no more type and file than a humming bird, and she would blab things about Willa she'd kept hidden from the team in Midshire EPS; it was a short step from spilling the beans about her Mensa membership to mentioning her photographic memory. Toni had to go – disappear – before Willa came back, that was all. She'd need to think about that...

SLATE

Claire Harris

"Do you have a minute?" Ellie asks as her shadow hangs over my desk. This doesn't sound like the normal chat request. Something more serious.

Without replying, I stand and reach for my stick and my bag. I follow Ellie as she walks through the open plan office to the glass fronted meeting rooms by the main staircase. She's walking quicker than me which means she has to wait a slightly uncomfortable amount of time holding the door open.

Oh. Shoku is here too. HR.

By the time we sit in our chairs I know what this is all about and I'm relieved. I want to laugh, but perhaps giggles aren't the right look for just now. It's today, I think. Finally, all the plans can begin. This is the domino I've been pushing for a while, and it's about to topple.

They look serious. Perhaps a bit nervous too. Seconds tick by punctuated by the rustling of paper and click of a ballpoint pen poised for action. Their body language is fascinating. They're deliberately avoiding each other. It's an interesting power play. I wonder what they're trying to make me feel.

A few more seconds pass – I'm happy to wait.

"Look," Ellie draws a big breath. "We know. We know what you've been up to."

Finally, she's said it. I see Shoku start to open the folder. Right, how should I play this? Innocent? Confused? Amused? Shocked? Angry? I didn't realise there would be so many choices in the moment. Of course, I've had a while to rehearse, and I took advantage of it.

I go for straight.

"I don't know what you mean," I say almost imperiously.

Vaguely, I wonder who the good cop is. I'm sure it won't be long before I find out. I think they were expecting a denial, but the tone of it has surprised them a little. They almost look at each other – almost.

"The money. The money is gone," Ellie says very calmly.

I really feel like I'd like to wind her up. Make her angry. A little payback for being such an ableist bitch.

"Which money? The coffee money? The Charity Box money? The money in general?" I'm feeling pedantic – I think they might have worked that out.

"No. The production budget over the last 15 months," says Ellie patiently.

"Not the coffee money then?" I persist.

"No," Ellie says firmly.

"Which productions?" I ask.

"All of them. All the ones you worked on," Shoku says rather less patiently.

"Is this the point at which you calmly reassure me that everything is OK and I'm not in any trouble?" I ask.

"No, I don't think so," says Shoku, shaking her head.

"We've got evidence," says Ellie.

They're a tag team now.

"Ah right." I'm still calm. I'm hoping to upgrade it to infuriatingly calm in a minute.

"This evidence, right here," Shoku says, picking up the folder she's been holding and starting to wave it a little.

"OK," I say casually.

I sit waiting for their next move.

"Is this the part where you tell us it was nothing to do with you and you don't know what's going on?" Ellie asks.

I let this pause become a little bit testy. I can see my non-cooperation is starting to piss them off. So now I'll change tactics.

"No. I know exactly what you're talking about. I noticed it too. I thought it was quite strange all that money disappeared so easily," I said, emphasising the last two words.

"What?" says a slightly shocked Ellie and not a little confused at my implication.

"You knew about it, and you didn't come to tell us?" Shoku continues.

"Well, I wouldn't, would I? Not since I was the one taking it. I'm really surprised it took you this long to notice."

Boom! They weren't expecting that. There are some goldfish mouths going on.

I reach inside my bag to pull out my own sheaf of papers. Honestly, I've been walking around with these for weeks waiting for this meeting.

The room is still silent.

"I would like to formally confirm to you that I have not been stealing money from the department."

Shoku's file is opening again. She starts to speak, but I interrupt her and point to my own papers.

"If I can draw your attention to this spreadsheet," I say.

"The 2023 production slate with associated budgets and expenditure?" Shoku confirms.

"Yes, as the title says. I'd like now for you to look at the sheet here," I continue.

Ellie is confused – "You've pulled up the slate from a decade ago."

"Absolutely," I agree. I've decided to do this bit in an over-scrupulous manner. "What do you notice?" I ask.

I can wait. They compare one sheet with another, pull out their own records and look them through. It takes a while, but there's some pointing and the ballpoint pen finally does some work drawing circles around figures. I thought I'd made it pretty obvious, moving the sums in whole amounts.

Some more assessing, pointing, inhalations of breath and they're there. The penny drops. There are some incomplete vocalisations from both of them, and then:

"But why the actual fuck would you do that?" Ellie screams.

"I'm beyond understanding; I'm completely shocked," Shoku is slightly more controlled, but that's because she doesn't know me as well.

"I see you've just confirmed the money is all present and correct. Just in a different place." I start to stand. "I'll leave these for you. I won't need them anymore," I say.

Ellie and Shoku sit slumped in their chairs with the dazed look of people who are trying to work out if it's better to follow me out of the room asking questions, or whether to just leave it.

I'm not going to say anything anyway.

I walk over to my desk and pack my things. There's not much – my pad, a couple of mechanical pencils and my travel coffee cup. In 10 seconds, I'm away to the lifts, waving at a few people giving me puzzled looks, and then I walk out of the building.

And that's how I sabotaged my career. But I had a good reason. I needed to escape, and I needed it to look like I'd been pushed.

SCHOOLDAYS

Glenise Borthwick

I had never quite made the transfer to keeping my daily schedule and notes online. It had to be more tactile, more an extension of myself, real and visible.

Every day it was my support mechanism ready to prop me up for another day at school. It was the first thing I touched in the morning and the last thing I put away into the dark recesses of my bag. It was always with me, back and forth, on my journey of resentment to school and my journey of relief on my way home.

The book became my diary and each day I noted the trivial and traumatic.

Each year I had a new one of these blank notebooks, the cover always cheerful with a witty saying on the front or a cartoon character. It was colourful and bright as I always intended my days to be.

Each day in school it lay amongst half chewed pencils, post-it notes creating a rainbow of things to do and a class dictionary open at a page that needed some delicate cleaning work to remove the obscenities that persisted.

It fought for a place amongst the detritus of my school day.

The contents read like volumes of my life: the highs and the lows, the ridiculous and the absurd. Neat lists alongside notes written so viciously that they went through three pages, deep red pen marks like slashes through great ideas.

Notes were made on lessons that had me cry and my pupils cry out in frustration. Lessons that had caused such engraved expressions of boredom and despair on my pupils' faces that I would never venture to teach them again. Pages folded over to hide errors of judgement from particular lessons, hidden as part of my shame. Notes had proliferated in the margins. The great ideas, accompanied by a glass or two of wine the night before, turned into lessons absurd and insane in equal measures.

It was the very first thing I looked at on arrival, my 'sat nav' for getting through the day. It consoled me and soothed me whilst the hoards entered my room and destroyed my silence and my patience.

Alongside the class information were my preferred lessons. Often repeated over to the next day as I strove to make a point, my pupils failing to see any.

I could hear it asking questions of me. The same questions I always asked myself. Instead of comments at the end of a pupil's work the same comments would reference my own lesson choices. Could do better, try to be more imaginative, make more of an effort.

Often I hoped to open the book and there, appearing like some sort of magic, would be a fresh idea, a fabulous lesson that would turn pupils into writers or into insightful critics. I wanted them to engage with the work, to treasure every word I uttered, but I was always upstaged by the weather, by the girl in the back row howling over her most recent failed romance or by an intervention to separate two boys and one very sharp pencil. There was always drama in the room but not in the lesson.

One particular lesson was finally abandoned as it took second place to the unfortunate demise of two Labradors, favoured pets of pupils. We all had to deal with the tears and eventually skipped the chapter in our novel *Of Mice and Men* where the dog was shot. Emotions like a Mexican wave often overwhelmed my lessons. Great literature was often halted to cope with the trauma suffered by 14-year-olds.

Over the terms there had appeared a list of pupils in my book who had annoyed or frustrated me. The ones who never had a pencil, who never stopped talking, who managed to leave graffiti but no evidence of their involvement in it. The magicians in the room who stole the drawing pins but managed to have the poster stay in place until they had left the room when it would flutter down and be stood on by the incoming hordes who showed little respect as it lay tattered and torn.

There were, in fact, days when the magic in the room was spectacular. Blu tac and Sellotape disappeared in front of my eyes, dictionaries were defaced and class texts subjected to feats of origami that turned Shakespearian worksheets into frogs and swans in equal measure. I never ceased to wonder that, in hindsight, that was probably their best outcome for many pupils.

Reminders to update my stationery needs were entered daily into my book. Somehow the pupils knew if I was holding out on them and if I actually had a pencil left in a drawer or in my bag. I could never outsmart them and caved in to their needs. Their gaze often pierced my very soul.

There were days when worksheets were turned into planes and missiles that would have astonished NASA with their intricacy and planning. I could never see the launch pad nor the pilot but had suspicions, always suspicions. When the crime scene grew cold, I would give up and try and catch the invisible culprits another time.

The class stood firm and no-one would tell. I could never crack them despite my devious ploys to do so. In my book, I noted down the suspects.

Each day from each class would go down the names of those who had once again nibbled at my ego, worn down my resistance and had me chant the same phrases about their poor behaviour. My book noted it all. The same names, every day, the same names.

One boy made an heroic effort to follow me in my record of work for all five years of his time in the school. We both were exasperated that our expectations of each other never changed and we sparred on and off, both winning little victories. He managed to be untouched by great literature; I managed to prevent him from engraving his name on every desk in my room. Banksy would've been proud of his anonymity, but not his art work.

When he eventually left, we both felt we had unfinished business, yet he caught me unaware when he made an effort to come and say a final goodbye, gifting me his two pencils he said he would have no need for: a parting gift he said. I felt an unexpected tear on my face after he left the room, then laughed when I realised he was actually just returning my own pencils.

As the terms went by the book read like a list of characters who had come and gone, who had endured my lessons and who had taken me and their classmates to the very edge of reason.

These were specific pupils who earned a place in my margins on a daily basis. Their names were noted down in certain colours. An ascending colour chart of frustration.

Some names were written in red immediately, others fluctuated from green to orange. There was an unwritten code as certain pupils vied for a colour upgrade.

At the end of term and the summer reaching out in front of me, hopeful and refreshing, I would sometimes read through my book – initially for ideas of success for the new term. Then just scrolling through it for my own interest.

I laughed at the emoji stickers some pupils gave me as a way of expressing their feelings on my lessons. I coveted the one gold star and the two bright orange 'well done' stickers.

I looked at my own graffiti and the sad faces that lined up at the end of one difficult Monday afternoon.

Looking back on a particular day in term two I saw his name. I remembered waiting on a class coming in with homework due and ready to take to task a particularly noisy and resentful pupil.

The page was blank as was the next. These were the days that I couldn't write.

He hadn't come into class. His seat lay empty, his classmates subdued. They said he died of a brain tumour in his sleep.

My last words to him had been harsh, borne out of sheer exasperation with his actions.

But in my book he was still alive, his name recorded in various pages. He would remain there for the rest of the school year. A silent and challenging name. Every day I saw it and every day I heard a silence much louder than his wild days in my classroom. My book wasn't just a record, not just a list, not just a reminder, but a catalogue of emotion and people who would live on in my memory.

It was also a barometer of my own wellbeing. The stresses of Mondays and joy of Fridays.

It evidenced my life in miniature. Teaching was never going to be a career with long lunches and champagne receptions. It was lessons interrupted by heads bumping off desks as one by one they fell asleep to my soporific words. It was sports days standing in the rain, parents who could put the fear of God into you, and school trips that were little more than long, long bus journeys and sick bags.

Teaching was never a sprint but more of a marathon. I had to outlast everyone in the room. Senior pupils who found fixing their eyelashes more important than learning about metaphors, junior pupils who needed consoling when their favourite sharpener had gone missing, girls who were shocked by my fashion choices and boys equally shocked by my enforced seating plans.

Every day was a struggle as I mispronounced names that were the flavour for that year. Pupils were mortified and reprimanded me if I had a syllable wrong in the vintage wine that they had been named after and I spent a whole term having to hide my laughter when I had to shout at Beyoncé for tearing paper out of her jotter.

I struggled to keep my life private from the questions from pupils who had an insatiable interest in my life. They were always concerned about the state of my mug following their most recent lesson in biology on germs, concerned about my inability to work out the technology to show simple clips and most of all were fascinated with the contents of my own pencil case.

Paper clips and Tippex had an unhealthy fascination for them but often it was my only connection with them before they sulked back to their seats to continue with their indifference to my lesson.

I was not the only teacher in the school who had a physical record of work. Technology had its place but we all had our paper copies which we often threw down on the table in the staff room to announce our arrival and exasperation. We knew when one of our colleagues had misplaced theirs as they stood rigid and unable to continue their day.

We all felt their pain as we hugged our own tighter.

The staffroom was our refuge where we shared concerns. Throwing open our records of work to chant names of those who persisted to invade our peace. Same pupils, same issues. We often huddled in our groupings in the staffroom, the Hobnob club, the card sharps, the food connoisseurs, all with one question. How many days of term left?

Yet the note books were more, so much more than a record of work or an aide memoire.

There were days when my pupils' results came in and we all broke into the biscuit tin and shared their delight and my own utter relief. There were days too when I had to console and encourage. Days when a sudden expression of understanding lit up their faces when the intricacies of the semicolon were realised.

They became the very evidence that, in even small ways, I had tried to make a difference, often against all odds.

Despite all of the issues in teaching, I was there because I cared.

LUNCH

Claire Harris

I've chosen my second-best coat. It's only Edward, but this new home has got a fancy restaurant. Something for the residents, he said, to make them feel like they're at a hotel instead of waiting to die. I'd laughed. Edward never waits for anything.

Standing at the hall mirror, I wonder about the new lipstick. I splashed out, upgraded my usual for a more upmarket brand. Actually, I wouldn't know. It was more expensive, though, if that means anything.

He's in the day room.

"Just down there," I'm told by a jaunty looking teenager behind reception.

It really is like arriving at a hotel. The last place had an unmanned side table at the entrance, a visitors' book that looked as though it had been there since the 70s and a selection of pens that didn't work.

When I get there, he's educating anyone within earshot on the intricacies of a command economy. They have those awful high-backed, fake leather armchairs with wooden arms that always remind me of hospital waiting rooms. The other occupants of the day room look like they might be waiting for someone to rescue them. And here I am. The angel of Oak House.

Edward spots me and smiles. He stands and we hug. Briefly.

At the restaurant there's a menu: fake leather cover like those chairs and a paper insert that doesn't quite fit under the corners.

"The salmon is usually good, or the soup," he says, with a wicked gleam in his eye.

"Cream of cauliflower with paprika," I say, reading aloud. "Oh no. No. I don't really think so."

He pointed out the soup deliberately. He knows I can't stand cauliflower. Never could, even when I was a child. It caused any number of arguments at home, but it just smells like toilet water, and I absolutely hate it. We resume the search for an acceptable starter.

Not finding anything immediately appealing I say, "May I ask you something, Edward?" I'm trying to convey an air of nonchalance, but it's been weighing on me. "I've been offered promotion to the position of office manager. What do you think?"

It's been hard going back to work after so long; I'm not where I thought I would be at 58.

"Terrific, Eleanor," Edward says. He looks up from his lunch deliberations. "What's the problem?"

I sigh and start to talk quickly, as if I just want to get it all out in one go without thinking too much.

"Well, on the plus side, I would get paid more money. Not millionaire levels, but still. Enough to allow me to achieve certain standards."

I don't really want much but it would be nice to move away from own-brand to mid-range and on a special day, perhaps, something from the '*Finest*' line. Or possibly an M&S cake for my birthday.

"On the other hand," I continued, "it would entail more work and responsibility. And the office is largely staffed by shirkers and idiots, Edward. It would be no easy matter, I can assure you, to manage them."

"I see your point," he says. "What you are asking is: is the extra money worth the extra hassle?"

"Quite," I agree. "You've summarised my problem very neatly."

I look up and our eyes meet briefly before we resume interrogating the menu. Garlic bread. Well, it's not as if I have to worry about kissing anyone.

THE WAIT

Angela MacGregor

Morag stood watching from the most westerly point of the land, scanning from the headland as far as the eye could see. She strained to catch just a tiny glimpse of the boat that would bring Hamish back to her. The wind lashed the torrents of rain, her wild hair whipping against her face, that same curly hair that Hamish loved so much. She searched the unforgiving waters, scanning and hoping. Her tears mixed with the rain on her face, as painful as the pounding within her heart. Fear gnawed into her being. She was desperate to have him back so that she could berate him for not listening to her. She had told him not to go. Pleaded with him. It seemed like an eternity ago when they woke up snuggled and safe together in their wee croft.

They had lovingly restored their home, from the abandoned mess that Uncle Dougal had left. He had set off to seek his fortunes away in the big city. Even back then Morag had the gift. She can still recall that day, running with all her might, gasping for breath but not daring to slow down. She knew she had to stop her uncle from leaving. The island was everything to her: it was safe, it was family and it was home. Her wild red curls bounced and buffeted about her face blinding her, yet still she did not slow down. Back then, she was sure footed and confident her legs could carry her at great speed.

As she reached the descent down to the harbour, she snatched a glimpse of those same red curls she knew so well. Gasping for breath she yelled out to her uncle. The wind snatched her voice and carried it across the moors. It was lost. Still, she didn't give in as she jumped every boggy ditch and stepped over every craggy rock that she knew so well. Finally, she got to the harbour and she begged him not to go, crying and gasping for breath as the panic set in. He was leaving. Why didn't he listen to her? Why? Why? Why?

A gust of wind punched the air from her lungs, snapping her from her reverie. She felt shock as she realised that she might have missed a clue on the darkening expanse of ocean on the horizon. Raising her arms in an attempt to protect her face she craned out seaward.

"Hamish! Hamish! Come home," she yelled, as once again the wind stole her voice.

She felt so guilty, as she worried about herself. How could she pay all the bills? They barely managed as it was. Did she even love Hamish or was that just selfish too? Another thought to scold herself with later, but not yet. Morag was resolute and determined to stay until the darkness finally descended, not wanting to go back home to another night without him. Selfish, selfish again, she said to herself, as the self-loathing set in. Later. Not now. She became increasingly helpless and desperate for Hamish to come home. Only he could soothe away all the demons that clawed and tore at her mind. Why had he not listened when she had begged him not to go? The light was all gone now.

"Another night without you," breathed Morag into the night.

A window smashed, sending a gust of wind in. Reaching under her shawl, chilling her to the bone, Morag gasped in the darkness trying to make sense of what was happening in her comatose state. Senses started to awaken as her ears could make out sounds, as if she was under water. "Ahhh," Morag yelled as she was at once blinded by lightning. In walked Katie.

Morag almost laughed in spite of herself. Katie had been Morag's friend since school. She was always the glamorous one. Living on the island, she always fought against the elements, keeping her perfectly coiffured hair in check. She was the first to get the latest fashions from the mainland back then and the storm she caused when she came to school with make-up on caused the local wifies to gossip. Ha! If they could see her now, laughed Morag. There in her living room stood Katie with a puce coloured face and her hair flung in every direction. Katie began her tirade at Morag: anger, fear, concern and relief etching its way across her once alabaster skin. Morag sagged and collapsed into darkness once more.

* * *

Morag stretched and yawned with a smile on her face, slowly waking from her sleep. Hamish was in the kitchen. She could smell the bacon and toast, mouth watering at the prospect. Keeping her eyes closed, she sighed lazily until she heard the footsteps coming into the bedroom. They were not Hamish's. She let out a gasp. It was Katie. How… what?

There was puzzlement, then the desperate realisation that Hamish was gone, the pain creeping its way back into her brain. She wanted to lay back down and crawl under the covers of darkness once more but she knew that would be useless against Katie's determination. Katie sat on the side of the bed, waiting. Obediently Morag ate the food without argument. Katie's relief was palpable.

It's been many years now without Hamish. Morag will often be seen, looking out over the headland of her beloved island. Not in desperation looking for Hamish but at peace with her love of her Island and the friendships that got her through.

DEDICATED FOLLOWER OF FASHION

Brian Devlin

I've never been particularly into 'scenes'. I liked looking at fashion and things but I never inhabited them. Well. Once I did. Only once.

Have you heard of the Bay City Rollers? Of course you have. Aside from whisky and haggis and kilts they were Scotland's most famous export for five minutes. They were jolly, and fun. They had a number of hits back in the day. "Bye, Bye, Baby", "Shang-a-lang." You must have heard of them? Anyway. They were great.

But what was particularly appealing was their gear. The Bay City Rollers were the epitome of fashion in my day. I longed to get dressed up in their baggy trousers – cut off above the ankles – but, get this: with a strip of tartan down the seam and at the turn-up at the bottom. Shirts too: black and shiny, but with a tartan collar and maybe a strip at the top of the breast pocket.

I pleaded for a pair of those trousers. I begged. Bartered. No chance. We had no money for nonsense like that. My social life at 16 was not especially exciting. On a Saturday it involved getting the bus from my village, Charlestown, up to the town, Dunfermline. Always on my own. I'd stand outside Woolworths for two hours on the steps, trying to look nonchalant. And then I'd wander down the hill to the lower bus stop to get the 5.05pm bus home. That was it. That was my youth. When, as a student, I lived in Frascati for a year, I regularly visited the Spanish Steps in Rome. I loved it. I adored watching the young men and women posing on the Steps. I suppose the two steps outside Woolies in Dunfermline was the Fife equivalent.

I was pissed off because one of my pals in the village did, in fact, get some of the Bay City Roller trousers. When I saw him wearing them what I meant to say was, "You entitled prick." What I did say was, "Oh, wow. You look great," as he slithered away with his new girlfriend at the Queen's Hall disco.

My mum, who was a home-help in the village, picked up on this trouser news. She picked up on ALL the news as she scooted from house to house on her wee red moped.

"Brian," she called one day. "Come here. See what I've got for ye."

She handed me a parcel that, curiously, she'd wrapped in left over wallpaper. I looked at her.

"For me?"

"Look inside."

I unwrapped the orange sunflower paper and there was a pair of Bay City Roller trousers. Sort of.

My mum was a great fan of jumble sales. She'd haunt them. Whenever a man in the village died I knew I'd be getting a new pair of shoes in a week or two.

I should have known what to expect to be fair. But even though my imagination was excessive I could never have conjured up this. They were indeed baggy trousers. But that's as far as the "Rollers" get-up went. Instead of the smooth 'stay-pressed' material I wanted, I was handed some brushed denim baggy jeans. There was tartan though – oh yes – she'd cut a three inch wide strip off a tartan skirt that she had snared at the latest jumble (one of the old ladies had recently popped her clogs) and had glued it on down the outer seam of the legs of the jeans. GLUED IT ON. I can still smell the chemicals.

"There you are now. That'll do you."

I looked at them. I looked at her.

"Thank your mum," my dad said.

I jumped. I hadn't seen him sitting in his chair by the fire watching the horse-racing on the television.

"Um…thanks very much."

I took the parcel up the stairs to my room and sat down on the bed with it beside me. It was 2pm. The bus was due at 2:45 to take me up to the town for my Woolworths sojourn. God, it was hot. I opened the window. So hot. The glue smell made my eyes water. Air. I needed air.

"Ah there now. Don't you look the height of fashion?"

"Thanks."

My dad was looking intently at Ceefax. Waiting for the listings and odds for the next race.

"Watch yourself up there now, Brian," he said.

He'd have said the same, with similar gravity, if I had been going to walk through the Tenderloin district of downtown San Francisco. But I was going to stand outside Woollies in Dunfermline for two hours. It didn't matter. A knife in the neck was a knife in the neck wherever you were.

I tried my best to ignore the sniggers, the whispered, 'Mother of Gods'. It was so blisteringly hot. Occasionally I smelled the waft of glue. I might have been a bit high, now I think of it. The "Hiyas" I made to people I knew were met with shocked looks. Hands over the mouth shock. I had no clue what was going on until one wee girl pointed to me and said to her dad, "what's wrong with that laddie's trousers?" I smiled. She clearly was too young to know the Rollers. Bless.

I glanced down and promptly threw up in my throat. In the heat the industrial glue that my mum had used to stick the dead woman's tartan strips onto my jumble sale denims had started to bubble and run. The tartan had slowly been unrolling and was curling up just above my knees leaving behind a runny diarrhoea-esque stripe down each leg of my trousers. I bolted. I ran down the hill to the bus station as fast as I could, the tartan stripes waving in the wind like streamers. People pressed themselves into building walls as I ran, not wanting to be splattered with whatever was emanating from my trousers.

Fuck you, Bay City Rollers. Showaddywaddy are better anyhow.

EMPTY CHAIR

INTRODUCTION

Angela MacGregor

It's not just ghosts who have unfinished business. As humans, we can all carry hurt or wounds from our past, whether emotional or physical. The "empty chair" exercise is part of Gestalt therapy and is a way for us to process our past safely. We put those we have unfinished business with in the chair – and talk to them. All the things we wish we'd said, we now get to articulate.

It's normal to carry scars. We all have them, but those scars are the evidence of wounds that are beginning to heal. Left unchecked, wounds can get infected. The empty chair is a way of cleansing and healing the emotional injuries we experience.

Many of the pieces in this chapter are anonymous, but in it, you will read our different ways of laying our past to rest, and learn where we are in the journey towards healing and wholeness.

I PLANTED A ROSE

I planted a rose bush when you died. Each time I walk past it, I bend my body forward to inhale its scent. I want to absorb it. The label said it was, "Nostalgia". It has pinky-white petals edged with red. It smells of summer and fresh rain. And roses. Not shop-bought ones that look pristine but smell of cardboard and plastic. Your rose smells of a perfect day, a freshly opened hardback book you've been waiting to read, an unexpected waterfall in the woods.

You loved roses. At least, I think you did. You never really said. Instead you told me what you didn't love. What you disagreed with. What you disapproved of.

The empty chair I imagine you'd want is upholstered with red velvet and gold brocade and richly embroidered with curlicues. A chair fit for a queen. Would it have been good enough? I wonder. Instead, I offer you an office chair. Anonymous. Unimposing.

Yes. I am angry with you. Since you died, things have gotten worse. You are not here to hate anymore. The things I hated about you became things to hate about myself. The people who knew you, now pretend you were wonderful. Just wonderful. No one mentions the times you criticised us all. The times you told your children, and your husband, they were wrong. The rushing, winding absences of love.

I wanted to know why you always said the world was a "dreadful" place. "Isn't the world a dreadful place?" you'd say over and over – like the full stop at the end of each sentence. It was rhetorical. Everyone should agree with you. We were commanded. I wanted to question you. But in your presence, all were silent. So I didn't. Instead, I started to see the world as dreadful. I allowed the algorithms in my head to blend with the algorithms in my newsfeed. War in Syria, children without families lost in the darkness of the care system, women dying slowly at the hands of their partners. All of it dreadful. All of it adding to the hate I felt for myself. I became a foul creature. Fit for nothing but the darkness of the soil.

But I found someone to save me. I was cocooned and safe in his arms. He was my protector. He saved me from my teenage self. From the disgusting creature I had always thought, deep down, that I was. I left her down there, buried in the peat bog and ran to him. There were wonders in him and he looked at me as if he had never seen such beauty. He looked at me as I look at your rose bush. With respect and awe. And I felt unbound. New. And I ran away with him, with the idea of him and me.

I remember you talked about a rose bush that had pricked your finger. Like a lady from a fairy tale. The injured finger was wrapped and treated with antibiotics. But the poison kept seeping into your bloodstream. Now you are dead, I see how that poison, from your childhood, your womanhood, must have bled into you. And how it infected your children. How that lovelessness, that empty yawning chasm, left unaddressed, sweeps everyone in its wake into an algorithm that beats with hunger and pain and hatred. An unstoppable beast.

You were sometimes kind. You knew I liked flowers. So you brought me fresh carnations, purple tulips, and bright brassy daffodils. And you gave gifts. But no love. Not really. And its absence took up so much space and oxygen I felt suffocated when you walked into a room. I wanted to offer you love but I couldn't. I started hating my coldness. I could see what you needed. But I couldn't give it. I couldn't even breathe, you see.

And now you are dead. We should speak kindly of the dead. But I cannot. For your poison has spread to me, and to the man who saved me. He is angry with you too. You are not here so his anger and pain stick to me like burrs. A thousand fold. So many they weigh me down. Weigh me so heavy I feel I am sinking back into the dark peaty soil I emerged from. And here I have to face myself – face the hated self I left behind so many years ago – the malignant troll of my teenage years. She is ugly, foul. A peat-brown bog girl, flecked with acne, deformed in shape – rotting. Yet, there is something in her that I cannot destroy. That I think I still love. Something of her in my own children who I love with a roaring passion.

And so I take her out of the bog. I hold her in my arms. Look into her mildewed eyes. Smell the rancour in her breath. And tell her with all my heart that she is loved. I turn the soil and gently mix the foul-smelling compost in my hands to feed your rose bush.

I put my younger self in your empty chair. It's a huge armchair now, with soft cushions. I wrap her in fine woollen blankets, and wipe the mud and grime from the pods of her eyes. And I see her beauty. And how much she wanted to be loved. And I bend my head to her and tell her she is loved.

And I go to the Nostalgia rose again. I crouch next to it in the rain and smell the past and present and think of the moments I missed that could have been filled with love. And I say I am sorry. Sorry to my younger self for hiding her in the depths, so her self-hatred was preserved in the bog. And sorry to you too because I could not staunch your wound. You never said sorry. But I can see now you were trying to bury your pain. I owe it to all my selves to forgive you.

IN THE NAME OF THE FATHER

Catriona Henderson

There always was a distance between us. Or perhaps not when I was a small child and didn't have annoying views and beliefs that didn't match yours. We may have been cut from the same cloth, though to a very different pattern.

I didn't choose your job or sign up to be a poster child for your work, and there were so many unspoken rules about what was and wasn't acceptable it was hard not to feel that I was always being judged. Did you have any idea just how pervasive the label of, "the minister's daughter" was as I grew up? How it followed me like a shadow, tapping into people's subconscious ideas of some saintly, religious child who bore little resemblance to me.

Not that I was a bad child, or even badly behaved. But when everyone around you has their own illogical expectations of everything you do and what you should know, based on a title that has been bestowed on you because of what a parent does, it is impossible to live up to that. Whatever I did, someone wasn't happy with it. And you were always so worried what other people thought, I was judged not only by your standards but by your fears of everyone else's too. I grew up in a fishbowl, inspected from all angles and at all times, and viewed through a different lens than other children.

For some reason, I was expected to know everything about the bible. No-one thinks children of electricians should know how to rewire a plug, never mind a house, by the time they are five, but by the time I started primary school there was an unspoken requirement for me to have encyclopaedic biblical knowledge. That was a horrible catch-22 situation: if I did know something it was taken as proof that I spent my evenings diligently studying the bible; if I didn't then I was automatically a failure. Swot or disappointment. That's not much of a choice for a child.

Things that were simple for other people became a fraught tightrope of balancing a clamour of critical opinions. It wasn't enough to appease you that I grudgingly came to church. More often than not, there was something not right about my clothes or my hair, something your god apparently wouldn't like. One day I heard you complaining to someone that I was wearing jeans. Jeans! Your god had supposedly seen death and destruction since the beginning of time, witnessed wars and disasters. Surely jeans were the least of their concerns. Not in your view. Or, more precisely, you were worried that your parishioners wouldn't approve so you made sure yours was the first voice to publicly castigate my sartorial choices. That was the day I decided beyond any doubt that the church was not my home. "Let he who has not sinned cast the first stone" was something that clearly didn't apply when judging your own child. In return I judged you harshly because of that, and our mutual disrespect for each other's views grew into an impassable crevasse in which our differences festered.

Growing up, I could see that other people's parents came home from work and got on with the rest of their lives. For you, that was impossible, concerned as you were that if people saw you doing something that wasn't work they'd think you were skiving. God may have had a day of rest, but not you. So even when you were being my dad, you were always still the minister. It was as if your clerical collar stayed round your neck permanently, whether visible or not. A dog collar indeed, relentless in its hounding of our family. Maybe that's another of the reasons I have no time for your god; servicing him made sure you rarely had time for me. I never told you how resentful I was that I also had to pay the penance of wearing that collar simply by my association with your job. My feelings were never of interest to you because they weren't as important as what other people thought.

Just as you never let yourself relax from the confines of your job title, I was never allowed to be anything other than the minister's daughter. The dual label of your job and my relationship to you seemed to be the first, and often the only, thing you and other people saw. It was like stepping into a new life when I left home, and people recognised me in my own name and not as a sub-set of you. Liberty at last; suffer the little child no more. I wonder if you sensed my deliverance and wished you, too, could be free.

I TOLD YOU

I told you, I TOLD you, and you did nothing.

Uncomfortable in that silence, your annoyance in the air, you… just couldn't be arsed. It took me weeks, no months, to build the courage to tell you, and you… did… nothing. I don't get it. Why didn't you react, do something, anything? Well almost nothing… ha… you made it worse, didn't you? Had to protect them, eh?

From that moment in time, I lived in fear. Not one person ever asked if I was ok. I wasn't. I wished for just one person to notice me: the teacher at school; my various sports coaches; just anyone to have been there for me. But no one was. And so it carried on.

I react in fearful ways now. I don't trust. I see all my inadequacies daily. In fact, I wear that pain, see that look, and breathe that darkness you let live, daily… And that's all from your decision at that point in time to do very little. YOU didn't listen to ME! You didn't want to know. Why didn't you help me? Why have I never been good enough? You said you loved me, but how could you have?

Over the years, you shaped my mind with these inadequacies about what a woman should be. Your chauvinistic ways, making me think my body was only going to be for the pleasure of men, like that porn you watched. Or that time you made me watch a film about a hooker so I could see what it would be like. I shouldn't have seen that. My eyes aged in a few seconds that day, thinking that I wouldn't be loved unless I looked like that. I was 8 years old ffs!

By God, YOU have a lot to answer for!

Looking back now, I actually feel physically sick about it all. How could I have grown up in such a screwed up atmosphere? And nobody saw, nobody helped, nobody even asked… now my mouth is tightly bound shut. I will never speak the truth about this.

However, I do say to you… Why was I not good enough? Why didn't you love me? You only cared when I was winning or achieving. You've been the same damn way through my whole life. If I'm not achieving, I ain't worth shit to you.

For years that hurt and I'm sure it will forever, but do you know what? I'm ok. I'll be fine. I'll lock it all away in that special place in my head, which should never have been opened. Because let's face it, if I ever did ask you I'd be disowned, cast out and worse off than now.

So, instead I'm choosing to distance myself from **you** and **your** darkness, that **you** bring to me.

I choose to say goodbye... I wish you well, knowing I'll never be able to build up the courage again to speak to you about this. And guess what, even though I grew up in that dark place, I don't wish you pain. Just, goodbye. I'll be civil as always but know this, inside I'm burning. You are the parasite in my life.

My eyes are wide open now! I'll see what others don't and I can and will help those who need it, I promise.

I will **NOT**... become... you!

LETTER TO DAD

I haven't spoken to you for a while. I'd like to tell you how things are for me since you died. One of my friends has cancer and when they told me, I thought of you, and the people who suffered at the hospital with you.

A few months after you died, the pandemic started. It was like the world had stopped. For me it had. The space was good at first; I needed it. Then the loneliness crept in. Things opened up, and things closed down, then opened up again. I left my ex. I was on my own, grieving my ex and grieving you.

As things opened up for good, I realised I didn't know who I was anymore and I started to panic.

I wasn't very well for a while. I struggled to talk to people, or at least, I didn't feel I had people to talk to. Everyone was having a hard time; it was difficult to find space to speak. I tried dating, which was exciting, getting to know new possibilities, but it was also painful. I was put on a pedestal a few times, only to be knocked off and shut out when they realised they couldn't fix me.

I moved several times in one year. I was frightened and unsettled, looking for a home. I kept reaching out to people who didn't really know me, panicking, looking for the reassurance you once gave me.

I bought a flat. I had barely decided to look into buying, but I liked it; I went for it. The walls were cracked and filled with soot; there was no heating; a crisp breeze blew through a gap in the living room window; the door frame fell off the first time I tried to close the front door; and I had a cold shower for several days until I could figure out how the pump worked.

Over the past year, I have been working on my flat, and with every room that's fixed, I feel like I'm healing. I like being able to close the broken wooden door, and be in my own space. The walls are now painted bright colours, the windows are fixed, the shower is warm and slowly, slowly, work is being done. The door frame is still hanging off, but I am getting to that. It is my home.

I don't think you would have imagined it of me – renovating my own flat – but it's helped me grow, and I have space to grieve. I've met someone too, who holds my hand, and is helping me rebuild my life.

I wonder if this is the life you would have wanted for me; I know you expected great things. I still see the hospital ward in my dreams. I follow those white corridors all the time in my mind. I am trying to be at peace, which is the most I can do for now.

ABSENT CHILD

Anthony S. Holroyd

This piece was written to a child I never had. Some years ago a partner of mine became pregnant. She decided, as is her right, to terminate the pregnancy. I did not want her to, but I respected, and continue to respect, that it was her choice to make and not mine. Nonetheless, I was deeply hurt and upset by the decision she made, and I still feel it was the wrong decision, made for the wrong reasons.

This exercise allowed me to vocalise some of the anguish I felt. I view it very much as a walk through the grieving process. At times, I felt and thought quite angry, and quite ugly, things. I am not proud of those thoughts but I do take ownership of them. To fail to include them here would be dishonest, and would mean painting myself in far too positive a light. This piece might be difficult reading for some, but that's only because it made for difficult writing. Writing this piece was an upsetting but deeply cathartic exercise. I finally felt I'd gotten things, "off my chest". The sense of closure I get from reading it back now is deeply welcome.

Absent Child

Protestations

But the chair is empty. There's no one there. Even the person I want to speak to isn't there. They never were really. They never were. More of an idea I suppose – a could be – a never was. And if they're there now? That chair's too big for them anyway.

Apologies

I'm sorry. I'm sorry you're not here, I still wish you were. I still think about how happy I might have been with you in my life. Stressed? Sure. Clueless? Naturally. Poorer for my troubles? Almost certainly. But happy. I would've given you all of me – I hope you know that. I would've broken my back to give you every chance I could . . .

Accusations

But she had to give you a chance first – and that was asking too much. I was always the stronger one. I was always the one who could rationalise; make sense of; make things seem not so bad. I was the one who could carry us both. Maybe I needed to be stronger – strong enough for three instead of two.

Excuses

I tried. Please know that I tried.
  I came up short.
  I couldn't get through to her.
  I couldn't change it.
  It wasn't my decision to make.

It never could have been – it never can be.
I don't blame her – I try not to anyway.

Lamentations

But God! I wish it could've been my call. I know why it couldn't be. Given my time again, I still wouldn't have stopped her. But God, I wish I could have – I wish I could have justified stopping her. I wish I could've abandoned every principle I have in exchange for you. I would have tried. We'd have been so happy.

Possibly.

I think.

Reality

But I'll never know you.

We never got the chance.

That chair is too big.

That chair is empty.

THE (VERY) EMPTY CHAIR

Neil Keay

You sit there in this open space
Inviting a response
A doorway to the past I think
My saviour or my nemesis
Reminding me of things long dead
I'd wanted them forgotten
An open wound
A painful thought
Not visiting again

I've said my piece
To those I loved
When they were on this earth
And others who have done me wrong
Don't get a second breath
We all have darkness in our life
And in the past I've faced it
Some skeletons stay locked away
Forever banished to the past
To some you are a helpful prop
To me you're just an empty chair

HELP PAGE

If you are struggling with issues raised in this book and would like help, here are some organisations to contact.

Samaritans
116 123

Scottish Women's aid
Domestic abuse
0131 226 6606

SARCS
Rape and Sexual Assault Support
0800 148 88 88

Cruse Bereavement Support
0808 808 1677

Scotland Support for Carers
0800 12 44 222

Cancer Support, Scotland
0800 652 4531

Breathing Space
0800 83 85 87

Printed in Great Britain
by Amazon

37857218R00142